Acting Edition

Raisin

Based on Lorraine Hansberry's
A Raisin in the Sun

Book by
Robert Nemiroff
and Charlotte Zaltzberg

Lyrics by
Robert Brittan

Music by
Judd Woldin

MUSIC AND THIRD-PARTY MATERIALS USE NOTE

Licensees are solely responsible for obtaining formal written permission from copyright owners to use copyrighted music and/or other copyrighted third-party materials (e.g. artworks, logos) in the performance of this play and are strongly cautioned to do so. If no such permission is obtained by the licensee, then the licensee must use only original music and materials that the licensee owns and controls. Licensees are solely responsible and liable for clearances of all third-party copyrighted materials, including without limitation music, and shall indemnify the copyright owners of the play(s) and their licensing agent, Concord Theatricals Corp., against any costs, expenses, losses and liabilities arising from the use of such copyrighted third-party materials by licensees. For music, please contact the appropriate music licensing authority in your territory for the rights to any incidental music.

IMPORTANT BILLING AND CREDIT REQUIREMENTS

If you have obtained performance rights to this title, please refer to your licensing agreement for important billing and credit requirements.

RAISIN was first presented on Broadway by ROBERT NEMIROFF at the 46th Street Theatre on October 18, 1973, with the following cast:

(In order of appearance)

PEOPLE OF THE SOUTHSIDE .... *Loretta Abbott, Elaine Beener, Glenn Brooks, Walter P. Brown, Karen Burke, Paul Carrington, Herb Downer, Mariyln Hamilton, Don Jay, Eugene Little, Marenda Perry, Al Perryman, Zelda Pulliam, Renee Rose, Ted Ross, Chuck Thorpes, Gloria Turner.*

PUSHER	*Al Perryman*
VICTIM	*Loretta Abbott*
RUTH YOUNGER	*Ernestine Jackson*
TRAVIS YOUNGER	*Ralph Carter*
MRS. JOHNSON	*Helen Martin*
WALTER LEE YOUNGER	*Joe Morton*
BENEATHA YOUNGER	*Deborah Allen*
LENA YOUNGER (MAMA)	*Virginia Capers*
ALTHEA	*Elaine Beener*
BOBO JONES	*Ted Ross*
WILLIE HARRIS	*Walter P. Brown*
JOSEPH ASAGAI	*Robert Jackson*
PASTOR	*Herb Downer*
PASTOR'S WIFE	*Marenda Perry*
KARL LINDNER	*Richard Sanders*

Scenery Designed by ROBERT U. TAYLOR; Costumes Designed by BERNARD JOHNSON; Lighting Designed by WILLIAM MINTZER.

Musical Director & Conductor HOWARD A. ROBERTS; Orchestrations by AL COHN, ROBERT FREEDMAN; Vocal Arrangements by JOYCE BROWN, HOWARD A. ROBERTS; Dance Arrangements by the Composer; Incidental Arrangements DOROTHEA FREITAG.

Associate Producers SYDNEY LEWIS, JACK FRIEL; Production Stage Manager HELAINE HEAD; Stage Managers NATE BARNETT, TONY NEELY; Production Associates IRVING WELZER, WILL MOTT, CHARLES BRIGGS.

Original Production by ARENA STAGE, Washington, D.C., by Arrangement with ROBERT NEMIROFF.

Production Directed and choreographed by DONALD McKAYLE.

In 1974, RAISIN won the Antoinette Perry (Tony) Award as Broadway's Best Musical, with nominations in nine categories: Best Musical, Best Score, Best Book of a Musical, Best Director, Best Actress, Best Actor, Best Supporting Actress, Best Supporting Actor, and Best Choreographer.

In 1975, composer Judd Woldin and lyricist Robert Brittan won the Grammy Award for Broadway's "Best Musical, Best Songs and Show Album" (Columbia Records).

In 1975–76, RAISIN was recommended as an entertainment "must" by the American Revolution Bicentennial Administration. And when the production finally closed on Broadway in December 1975, RAISIN embarked on an 18-month first class National Tour of forty major cities in the United States and Canada. In most of these, "RAISIN Week" or "RAISIN Month" was proclaimed by the mayor and/or governor to coincide with the opening: in many, RAISIN set attendance records; and in some, it was the first Broadway production to appear in decades.

In all, RAISIN was attended by some 3½ million people.

The National Company of RAISIN, at one time or another, included the following:

THE CAST

PEOPLE OF THE SOUTHSIDE ...... *H. Douglas Berring, Cynthia Brown,*
Jacqueline Derouen, Charliese Drakeford,
Charles E. Grant, Sheila Holmes, Eddie Jordan,
Cleveland Pennington, Lacy Darryl Phillips, Martial Romain,
Henry Shaw, Michael Smith, Corliss Taylor, Renee Warren
PUSHER .... *Keith Simmons/Le'von Campbell*
VICTIM .... *Loretta Abbott/Bonita Jackson*
RUTH YOUNGER .... *Mary Seymour/Vanessa Shaw*
TRAVIS YOUNGER .... *Darren Green/Altyrone "Deno" Brown*
MRS. JOHNSON .... *Sandra Phillips/Emme Kemp*
WALTER LEE YOUNGER ...... *Autris Paige/Gregg Baker/ Nate Barnett*
BENEATHA YOUNGER .... *Arnetia Walker*
LENA YOUNGER (MAMA) .... *Virginia Caspers/Sandra Phillips*
BAR GIRL .... *Zelda Pulliam*
BOBO JONES .... *Irving Barnes*
WILLIE HARRIS .... *Walter P. Brown/Roderick Sibert/Ned Wright*
JOSEPH ASAGAI .... *Milt Grayson/Nate Barnett*
PASTOR .... *Roderick Sibert/Isaac Clay*
PASTOR'S WIFE .... *Kay Barnes*
KARL LINDNER .... *Stacy McAdams*

Production Stage Manager TONY NEELY; Production Supervisor NATE BARNETT; Stage Managers BURT WOOD, STACY MCADAMS; Musical Director & Conductor MARGARET HARRIS/JACK HOLMES/LEONARD OXLEY; Dance Supervision ZELDA PULLIAM.

General Manager JOHN CORKILL; Company Manager KIMO GERALD/ SHEILA PHILLIPS.

Executive Associates CHARLES BRIGGS, WILL MOTT.

MUSIC

The following orchestrations are available from Samuel French:

1. *The Full Broadway Orchestration:*
    Strings:
       1st & 2nd violins; viola; cello
    Reeds:
       #1—soprano and alto sax/clarinet/flute/alto flute/piccolo
       #2—alto sax/clarinet/flute/alto flute
       #3—tenor sax/clarinet/flute/alto flute
       #4—baritone sax/bass clarinet/clarinet
    Brass:
       trumpet 1 & 2 & 3/fluegelhorn; trombone 1 & 2; horn; tuba
    Rhythm:
       1 piano; 1 Farfisa organ; 1 guitar; 1 acoustic bass/fender bass;
       1 drums; 1 percussion; 1 African drums
2. *Smaller orchestration without strings:*
    Reeds:
       #1—soprano and alto sax/clarinet/flute/alto flute/piccolo
       #2—alto sax/clarinet/flute
       #3—tenor sax/clarinet/flute
       #4—baritone sax/bass clarinet
    Brass:
       same as above.
    Rhythm:
       1 piano/Farfisa organ; 1 guitar; 1 fender bass; 1 drums; 1 per-
       cussion
3. *Bus and Truck Version,* scored for 8:
    Rhythm same as smaller orchestration; 1 trumpet/fluegelhorn; 1
       trombone; 1 reed (soprano, tenor and baritone sax/clarinet/flute.)
       (Same books as above except for fender bass, trumpet, trombone,
       and reed, for which separate books are available.)

All three of these versions can be conducted from the master con-
ductor/keyboard book.

CHORAL/PRINCIPALS BOOK of the songs is available.

The RAISIN SONG FOLIO is published by Blackwood Music, Inc.,
and is available through Big Three Music. These are simplified arrangements, good for learning purposes but keys, tempos and arrangements
are not necessarily the same as in the orchestration.

CONTENTS

MUSICAL NUMBERS

ACT ONE

ACT TWO

PRODUCTION NOTES*

I. THE SETTING

There is no curtain.

As the audience enters the theatre, it sees the RAISIN set illuminated with cool green and blue lights. It is a black and grey-toned multi-leveled structure backed by a brick wall, representing, at first glance, the concrete and asphalt ghetto of Southside Chicago. It is scarred, dangerous and tender with things blending and shifting back and forth the way they do in real life. This is the place Black people refer to when they talk about the Block.

As if by magic—as the muted brick backdrop shifts to brilliant red, becomes a field of moonlit blue, pulsates with the greens of mythic jungles or the golds of summer sundowns—the singular, multi-leveled set can be instantly transformed from a bustling street to an apartment, a rollicking soul bar, a sanctified Church on Sunday morning.

Set changes are easily executed by the cast through the use of a few items of furniture and a series of small mobile platforms (which make into beds, church benches, bars) hinged to the stage floor for accurate and quick positioning. A balcony begins downstage right (D. R.), stretching up right (U. R.) and across the upstage area, and leading off left (L.). Several stair units lead off and onto the balcony.

This fusion of platforms, translucent flats and balconies, windows and entranceways, combines to symbolize the stifling, inhuman conditions of ghetto life which surround and contain the family of Walter Lee Younger.

A table, two chairs and a rocking chair—all the same color and simplified block construction as the set—when positioned on the slightly raised area from center (C.) to left (L.), create the family's combined livingroom/kitchenette. A bench unit becomes the sofa. A folding bench unit becomes the make-down bed on which TRAVIS sleeps. Behind this, the somewhat higher platform up center (U. C.) becomes WALTER and RUTH's room (with a mobile unit as their bed). MAMA and BENEATHA share a third, unseen room off left.

The platform edges at center mark the front door and, at right angles to it, the door to WALTER and RUTH's room. Up center left (U. C. L.), a step marks the back door to the hallway that leads to the bathroom the Youngers share, off left, with a neighbor, MRS. JOHNSON, who lives further up the hall, off left.

Downstage left (D. L.) there is a small railing which, when we are in the apartment, becomes a windowsill on which sits an undernourished little potted plant—MAMA's only link with the sunlight and green vistas of the home she left, nearly forty years before, to come North to Chicago.

* Also see "A NOTE ON FUTURE PRODUCTIONS," p. 101.

II. FURNITURE AND PROPS

Apart from the above items and a few carefully selected props, everything else in the apartment and the play is imagined: created in the mind's eye of the audience by pantomime.

Floorplans for the exact placement of the furniture in the apartment and other locales are on pp. 113–16, along with a diagram indicating the presumed location of doors and windows, closets and pantries, major household appliances and other objects that exist only in pantomime.

The props are the following: personal items, the plant, the partnership contract, WILLIE's pen, the box BENEATHA's robe and headwrap are brought in, an African necklace, the insurance check and envelope, a tambourine, an envelope of money, LINDNER's card, attache case, pen and contract of sale.

TIME: The Early 1950's

PLACE: Chicago, U.S.A.

What happens to a dream deferred?
Does it dry up
Like a raisin in the sun?
Or fester like a sore—
And then run?
Does it stink like rotten meat?
Or crust and sugar over—
Like a syrupy sweet?

Maybe it just sags
Like a heavy load.

Or does it explode?

—Langston Hughes

Raisin

ACT ONE

PROLOGUE

Night. The Block, Southside Chicago. A jazz ballet.

Music Cue I [Score #1]: *As the house and stage lights dim to black, the haunting wail of a soprano sax solo is briefly heard; as it gives way to the staccato driving rhythms of the orchestra, the Block materializes.*

From the deep blue shadows, cut by garish neon, two groovy CATS *with "do-rags" on their heads bop on,* U. L., *and across, making their fingerpopping way out for the night. At* D. R. C., *they give each other some skin (palm-to-palm hand-slap). One bops across* L., *greets the local* PUSHER, *a flashily dressed gent,* D. L., *then circles* U. *and off* R., *while the* PUSHER *meets the other,* R. C.

The two leap and greet each other with a jive ritual handshake, as a young CHICK *enters,* D. R., *checking her make-up for a date. The men dance in comment and follow as she circles sexily* U. L. PUSHER *exits while* CAT *follows her to* U. R. C., *and stands watching from the shadows.*

During this a DRUNK *has staggered on,* D. L., *in silent furious argument with the unseen bartender of a club from which he has just been thrown, off* L. *He sits to get himself together and watches hazily.*

A SECOND CHICK *joins the first, at* C., *and a foxy* THIRD *in a bright fuscia coat struts on, from* U. R., *showing off her new coat to her envious friends: as she exits they mimic and mock her. The music picks up tempo, a* FOURTH CHICK *and the* FIRST CAT *join them, from* U. R., *and all circle,* R. C., *in a jazz dance extension of a jitterbug boogie of the '50's. A young* FIFTH GIRL (*the* VICTIM), *passing by, joins in hesitantly and uncertainly—while the* DRUNK, *who has been weaving his way across* D. R., *tries vainly to interject himself and at last, giving up, staggers upstairs.*

At stage L. *the* PUSHER *prances out, stops, sits and snorts a spoon or two of coke. He sees the* FIFTH GIRL, *his* VICTIM, *and jack-knifes high in a leap before her,* D. R., *as the night people finish their business and hurry off into the fast-approaching dawn.*

Meanwhile, in the shadows of the R. *balcony above them, another drama has been soundlessly taking place*: The* DRUNK, *unable to find his keys, bangs on his tenement door and his irate* WIFE *answers, remonstrating. He starts back down at the sight of the* WOMEN *dancing below, but his* LITTLE BOY *appears and grabs his coat. The* WIFE *pushes the child back inside and hauls in her husband— while at another balcony door,* D. R., *a* HOUSEWIFE *comes out for the milk. She looks down, signals vainly for the attention of* DRUNK'S WIFE, *calls for her own* HUSBAND, *who presently joins her, and stands looking helplessly down at the scene below:*

As the music builds, PUSHER *and* VICTIM *have begun a dance of enticement, frenzied seduction and brutalization as he forces her to snort heroin. The* VICTIM *becomes dizzy, losing consciousness. The music crescendoes. She slides down his body, grabs his ankle and lies in a heap before him, as other* SOUTHSIDERS *pass by* U. S., *not seeing or caring to get involved. He casts her off, dances over her and—as the music crashes to a halt—leaps triumphantly off,* R., *in search of more victims.*

---

*This action is an added element of texture and should not, under any circumstances, detract from the dance of PUSHER and VICTIM occurring below.

After applause—Music Cue II [Score #1A]: *underscoring.*

The HOUSEWIFE *and her* HUSBAND *rush down and, as the music
    resumes, drag the semi-conscious* VICTIM *upstairs to
    safety, while the Block melts away and daylight sneaks
    up on*—

ACT ONE

SCENE 1

The Younger family livingroom/kitchenette. Early morning.

WALTER *and* TRAVIS *have entered unseen during the Prologue and now lie sleeping on their respective beds. As the light comes up,* RUTH, *in a bathrobe, enters yawning from the bathroom. She crosses to the sink,* D. C., *and throws water on her face in an effort to wake up.*

RUTH. Walter Lee—it's after seven thirty! (*She crosses to* TRAVIS, *shakes him.*) Okay, Travis. Up! (*She stands him up, fast asleep, and crosses to the closet for a towel. He falls into a sitting position and then flops back into bed.*) Walter! It's time for you to get up! (RUTH *turns and sees* TRAVIS, *stands him up again.*) C'mon now, honey. You wanna get in that bathroom first, you better shake your little behind. Here— (*Hands him the towel.*) Come on. (*Steers him up onto the hall doorway landing, where he stands inert and unseeing.*) Walter Lee! (*As she starts towards the bedroom,* TRAVIS *topples backwards—on a sixth sense she turns, just in time, to catch him.*) Travis, honey, go on. (*Seeing the next-door neighbor,* MRS. JOHNSON, *towel in hand, shambling down the hall from* L. *in bathrobe and slippers.*) *Grab it!* And hold the door for your Daddy! (*As* MRS. JOHNSON *rounds the bend,* TRAVIS *springs to life and easily beats her to the bathroom. She shoots his mother a look;* RUTH *shrugs innocently and shuts the door.* MRS. JOHNSON *stops—and pleads with God for endurance.*)

MRS. JOHNSON. You saw 'em, Father. We supposed to share that bathroom. That family's always in there! (*She rounds the bend toward her room, then turns back for a parting shot through the door.*) And they ain't no *cleaner* when they come out! . . . (*Marches off* L. RUTH *crosses to the sink, gets a frying pan from underneath, puts it on the stove, and starts stirring oatmeal. Behind her back, as she talks,* WALTER *sits up and yawns, staggers out to the back door, peers blindly at the bathroom, and then comes back, stretching, as he surveys his wife's fine frame appreciatively.*)

RUTH. (*Busy at stove, she does not see* WALTER.) All right, man. You just stay in there and the next thing you know Travis be out and Mrs. Johnson be in that bathroom and you be cussing and fussing around here like a madman and be late, too. (RUTH *adjusts the flame, bending over, as, completely exasperated at his presumed lack of progress, she yells.*) Walter Lee! Walter Lee Younger—

WALTER. (*Tiptoes up playfully and embraces her from behind.*) That's my name, baby! (RUTH *warms for the merest moment.*) You look young this morning, baby. Real young. (*But abruptly she stiffens: she's not having any.*) Just for a second there you looked *so* fine. (*Drily, releasing her.*) It's *gone* now—you look like *yourself* again!

RUTH. (*Pleased in spite of herself, and slightly amused.*) If you don't shut up and leave me alone . . . (*Takes a bowl from the counter and sets it on the table.*)

WALTER. (*Crossing* c., *a plaint to the gods, saltily.*) You know, the first thing a man ought to learn in life is not to make love to no colored woman at eight o'clock in the morning. You all is some *eeeevil* people at eight o'clock in the morning! (*He crosses to back door. She breaks eggs into bowl, crosses to sink to dispose of the shells, and back to table.*)

RUTH. What kind of eggs you want?

WALTER. (*Looking out.*) Not scrambled. (*She immediately starts scrambling. He notes this with a helpless gesture to heaven, crosses over, stops her hand and takes her in his arms.*) Ruth, baby, you know after tomorrow you ain't gonna be standing around here fixing no eggs for me! (*He kisses her lightly.*)

RUTH. (*Pushing past him to the cabinet for a match. Drily.*) You done taken up cooking?

WALTER. You know what I'm talking about—

RUTH. (*Lighting stove.*) Now Walter, you just couldn't be talking 'bout that big old insurance check comin' to your mama tomorrow!? You know that ain't none of our money— (*She gets plates from an upper shelf—he takes them from her and sets them on the table.*)

WALTER. Mama'd listen to you. All you have to do is sit down with her like you do and say— (*Crosses to rocker and starts it rocking. Turning back and forth between his wife and "Mama" in the rocker, to demonstrate.*) "Lena, you know that store Walter Lee's just got his heart so set on . . ." Then you sip your coffee, see, and say, real cool, "I am sure Walter

Lee will make a killing and double your money back." (*A beat. To* RUTH.) Well, maybe don't say "killing"—I'm not so sure mama'd understand what that means . . .

RUTH. Now there ain't too much mama don't understand, Walter Lee . . . (*She sets the plates around the table.*)

WALTER. Well, then you explain to her about how it's all legal-like, the partnership—me and Bobo and Willie Harris—

RUTH. (*Automatically.*) Willie Harris is a good-for-nothing loudmouth. (*Gets the frying pan and crosses back to the table to dish out the eggs.*)

WALTER. (*Stung.*) Sure! Anybody I do business with has got to be a good-for-nothing loudmouth! Well, let me tell you something about Willie Harris—

RUTH. (*Abrupt dismissal.*) —he got a handful of "gimme" and a mouth full of "much obliged"! (*She crosses to sink to wash pan.*)

WALTER. Why? Cause he knows how to operate? Knows how to think big?

RUTH. Now, Walter, will you eat your eggs . . .

WALTER. Ruth, honey, this thing cannot wait forever and all I'm asking for you to do is to talk to mama—

RUTH. (*Overriding him.*) Walter, would you please leave me alone!

WALTER. (*A moment of silence. He crosses angrily upstage, then back to* RUTH.) Oh, you fed up, ain't you? Fed up with everything! But you couldn't do one thing to help!

RUTH. Walter, that money's from your daddy to your mama—

WALTER. My daddy would have wanted me to have this chance—

RUTH. (*By rote—automatic dismissal as she crosses away to cabinet.*) Eat your eggs, they gonna be cold. (*As* WALTER *turns hopelessly away,* D. L., *struggling to contain his anger, she gets cups and, as he continues, puts them on the table, then cream off the counter.*)

WALTER. (*Looking off, out front.*) Eat my eggs?! (Music Cue III [Score #2]: *MUSIC echoes ironically.*) Eat my eggs. (*It echoes again.*) Eat my eggs!!

song: "MAN SAY"

MAN SAY, "I GOT ME A DREAM!"
WOMAN SAY,—

(*Mimicking.*)
"PASS THE CREAM!"
(*Passes the cream to her. She turns away and putters busily about the kitchen ignoring him.*)
MAN SAY, "JUST HEAR THE PLANS THAT I'VE
    MADE!"
WOMAN SAY,—
(*Picks jar off a shelf and puts it down on the table—on the word.*)
"MARMALADE!"

MAN SAY, "DON'T MAKE ME WAIT!"
WOMAN SAY, "PASS YOUR PLATE!"
(*Moves a plate.*)
MAN SAY, "HERE'S WHAT I CARE 'BOUT MOST!"
WOMAN SAY,—
(*Picking up hot toast and burning his fingers.*)
"BURNT THE TOAST!"
(*She sits at table, R. chair, escaping into her coffee.*)
MAN SAY, "I GOTTA DO SOMETHING *BIG* 'FORE
    I GET TOO OLD!"
WOMAN SAY, "COFFEE'S GETTING COLD!"
MAN SAY, "WHEN THE CHANCE COMES BY,
WIN OR LOSE—
(*With passion.*)
GOTTA TRY!"
(*Indicating* TRAVIS'S *couch.*)
THAT BOY SLEEPING IN THE LIVING ROOM
NEEDS LIVING ROOM TO GROW.
TAKE A LOOK AROUND . . . WHAT DO YOU SEE?
(*Indicating the whole room.*)
IS *THIS* GONNA BE ALL HE'LL EVER KNOW?
(*As the MUSIC continues under.*)
   RUTH. Honey, you never say nothing new. I mean, so you'd rather be Mr. Arnold than be his chauffeur. So—I'd rather be living in Buckingham Palace!
   WALTER. (*Crossing back to her.*) And I'm telling you this ain't no fly-by-night proposition. We got a partnership—
   RUTH. Walter, eat your eggs. You gonna be late!
   WALTER.
MAN SAY, "LOOK OUT! DON'T TRY TO SLOW ME
    DOWN,
HERE COMES A *GIANT* FIFTY FOOT HIGH!"

MAN SAY, "NO THIS OR THAT!"
HE SAY, *"HERE'S* WHERE IT'S AT.
REACH UP! GRAB A PIECE OF THE SKY—"

(*The note hangs as she faces him. The MUSIC continues under—SAFETY VAMP.*)

RUTH. (*She crosses down to him.*) Now look, Walter Lee, your mama don't want you takin' no risks with that money—

WALTER. "Risks!" Here I'm trying to talk to you about me—about *us*—and all you can say is—

RUTH. Walter Lee, will you eat your—

WALTER. (*Exploding.*) DAMN MY EGGS DAMN ALL THE EGGS THERE EVER WAS!

RUTH. Then get dressed and go . . . to . . . work! (End SAFETY VAMP.)

WALTER. (*The silence of inexpressible frustration. Then, aut front, restraining himself, with deliberately exaggerated calm.*)

THERE'S THE ANSWER I BEEN LOOKING FOR.
IT'S CLEAR AS CLEAR CAN BE.
(*She sits back down, helplessly.*)
NOW I KNOW THE WAY TO MAKE THE GRADE:
(*Emphasizing the pun.*)
I'LL EAT WHAT'S BEEN *LAID*
'SPECIALLY FOR ME!
(*Facing her. Urgently.*)
MAN SAY, "RIGHT NOW! *THIS* IS THAT CHANCE TO MOVE,
NO TIME TO WALK, GET READY TO FLY!"
MAN SAY, *"LIFE'S* ON THE LINE!"
HE SAY, "IT'S *YOURS* AND *MINE!*
WAKE UP 'FORE IT PASSES YOU BY!"
WOMAN SAY, WOMAN SAY,
WOMAN SAY, "EAT YOUR EGGS!"
(*He sits in the L. chair.*)
Damn. (Music cut off.)

TRAVIS. (*Returning from bathroom, sees* MRS. JOHNSON *on her way again.*) Hurry up, daddy! (WALTER *runs to his room, grabs up various toilet articles, dashes out the door—and past* MRS. JOHNSON—*with a whoop.*)

MRS. JOHNSON. (*Stops, rocking on her heels from having*

almost been run over.) You my witness, Lord! Runnin' by me
like they on a racetrack— (*Starts back, then stops for a
parting shot toward bathroom.*) They either constipated or
they got diarrhea . . . (*She rounds the bend and exits* L. *During
this* RUTH *has moved the* D. R. *chair* U. S. *to the head of
table facing* D. S.)

TRAVIS. (*Making his bed, after closing the door.* RUTH *is at
the table setting utensils for his breakfast.*) Mama, this is the
morning the teacher say we supposed to bring fifty cents for
Negro History Week and—

RUTH. (*Crossing back to stove for the oatmeal.*) We ain't
got no fifty cents this morning.

TRAVIS. But, Ma, the teacher said—

RUTH. (*Pouring oats in bowl at table, then back to stove.*)
Now I don't care what teacher said! We ain't got no fifty
cents, so just hush and get over here and eat your breakfast.

TRAVIS. (*Crossing eagerly toward his grandmother's room.*)
Maybe grandma will give me that money . . .

RUTH. Travis Willard Younger! Sit down. (TRAVIS *stops
with a great sigh of oppression, comes to the table and sits,*
U. C. *chair.*) Your grandma's been gone since early this morning.

TRAVIS. (*Petulantly pushing his bowl away and resting head
on fist.*) I ain't hungry.

RUTH. (*Gently.*) I made you hot oats special.

TRAVIS. (*Makes a face—picks up his spoon, stabs the oatmeal, raises spoon and lets, first, the oatmeal, and, then, the
spoon drop back into the bowl from full height.*) It's too
lumpy.

RUTH. (*Pushes the bowl back in front of him.*) Now you
eat! (*As she crosses to the counter,* TRAVIS *shovels angry
spoonfuls into his mouth and throws the spoon down. He gets
up, crosses to couch, picks up his cap and jacket.*)

TRAVIS. I'm gone!

RUTH. You got your milk money?

TRAVIS. (*Sulking.*) Yes'm.

RUTH. And not one penny for no caps, you hear?

TRAVIS. Yes, ma'am. (*Furious, he throws his coat on.*)

RUTH. Here. (*She hands him a glass of milk. He takes one
sip and hands it back.*) Finish it! (*He downs the rest under
protest, wipes his mouth, hands back the glass, then heads for
the door, where he halts, arms folded and back to his mother,*

pouting. RUTH *folds her arms in precise imitation of him and broadly mimics.*) "Oh, Mama makes me so mad sometimes I don't know what to do!" (*She sneaks a look. He doesn't respond.*) "Hmph! I wouldn't kiss that woman goodbye for nothin' in this world! (Music Cue IV [Score #3].) Not for nothing in this world!"

SONG: "WHOSE LITTLE ANGRY MAN"

(*As* TRAVIS *struggles manfully to maintain his dignity. Gently teasing.*)
WHOSE LITTLE ANGRY MAN ARE YOU . . .
NOW LET ME SEE?
CAN I BE SURE THAT YOU BELONG TO ME?
(*She crosses to him. He side-steps crisply at the last possible moment and stalks* D. C.)
WHOSE LITTLE PUFF OF SMOKE AND FLAME?
WHOSE LITTLE ROAR OF MANLY THUNDER?
I WONDER, WHAT'S YOUR NAME?
(TRAVIS *rolls his eyes with disdain.* RUTH *follows him* D., *keeping her distance, then moves* D. L. *of the table.*)
MY LITTLE BOY WOULD NEVER BE AS MEAN AS
    YOU.
HE'D NEVER SAY GOODBYE WITHOUT A KISS
    OR TWO.
(*He has stolen a look at her and been caught.*)
I SEE YOU MAKING EYES AT ME
AND THAT'S AN OLD FAMILIAR SIGN.
(*Playfully.*)
I GUESS YOU'RE MINE.

(*MUSIC continues under.* RUTH *starts cleaning the table as* TRAVIS *marches to the door—then stops to try again.*)

TRAVIS. Mama, if I don't bring that fifty cents to school, I'm gonna be the most ignorant Negro about Negro History Week in the whole school!

RUTH. (RUTH *crosses to him pulling out comb—takes his cap off and hands it to him, and starts combing his hair. She's laughing and playful; he's fighting her, but playing too.*) . . . And the poorest, meanest, messiest, too! 'Bout to march out of here with that head looking just like chickens slept in it!

TRAVIS. Aww gaalee, Mama! (*As in, "I'm not a child any-more."*)

RUTH. (*Still mimicking him.*) "Aw . . . gaaaalllleeeeee, Mama!"

TRAVIS. Ouch! (*She has pulled a snarl in his hair; he jerks away, humiliated, rubbing his injured head, then puts his cap on—turning it manfully to the side—and folds his arms again.*)

RUTH.

MY LITTLE BOY WOULD NEVER BE AS MEAN
    AS YOU.

HE'D NEVER SAY GOODBYE—

(TRAVIS *starts for the door.* RUTH *stops him.*)

WITHOUT A KISS—

(*Kisses him.*)

—OR TWO.

(RUTH *tries to kiss him again, he eludes her and makes it to the door unscathed, implacable—but sneaking looks at her, too.*)

I SEE YOU MAKING EYES AT ME

AND THAT'S AN OLD FAMILIAR SIGN.

I GUESS YOU'RE MINE.

(*Music cut off. She holds out her arms—he runs into them and gives her a hug and kiss. She puts him down just as* WALTER *crosses into the bedroom to put his things away.*)

TRAVIS. (*New aggressiveness—in the presence of his father.*) Mama, can I *please* have the fifty cents for school?

RUTH. (*Very gently.*) Honey, I told you we ain't got it . . . okay?

WALTER. (*From the bedroom doorway. Outraged.*) Now what you tell the boy things like that for? (*Grandly reaching into his pocket and looking her in the eye.*) Come here, son . . . (TRAVIS *crosses to him.*) Here. (*Hands the boy fifty cents, eyes still fixed defiantly on his wife's.*)

TRAVIS. Thanks, Daddy. (*He starts out.* RUTH *watches them both with murder in her eyes.*)

WALTER. (*Reaching out and halting* TRAVIS *on an after-thought.*) In fact, here's another fifty cents! Buy yourself some fruit . . . or take a taxicab to school or something!

TRAVIS. (*Jumps up and hugs his father.*) Thanks, Daddy! (*Crosses to* RUTH, *gives her a kiss; then back to* WALTER, *gives him "five," palm to palm, and exits—triumphantly*

adopting the jaunty knee-dipping strut of the ghetto the mo-
ment he is out the door. WALTER *and* RUTH'S *eyes remain*
locked.)

WALTER. (*A beat. Defiantly.*) Now that's *my* boy.

(BENEATHA, WALTER'S *teenage sister, enters from off* L. *Yawn-*
ing, scratching her bottom, and generally "a sight" in
bedclothes and robe, her face a blob of cold cream, hair
a thicket of curlers, she has just awakened. She passes
through blindly and looks out at the bathroom at the
precise moment MRS. JOHNSON *again appears on her*
endless mission. The old lady sees BENEATHA, *jumps, gal-*
vanizes herself to a final effort and beats it to the bath-
room. BENEATHA *turns back with a sleepy vengeance.*)

BENEATHA. Well, there goes half an hour. That woman is
gonna give me a serious *kidney* condition! (*Scratching and*
yawning, she staggers D. L. *to lean against the windowsill.*)

WALTER. (*Surveys her clinically, then.*) You are one
horrible-looking chick at this hour.

BENEATHA. (*Drily.*) Well, good morning, everybody.

WALTER. (*Amused but interested. Senselessly.*) So how is
school?

BENEATHA. (*Sugar sweet, but the sarcasm builds, as she*
speaks, to a final sharp thrust.) Oh lovely. Lovely. And, you
know, biology is really the greatest. Yesterday I dissected
something— (*Looking up at him.*) looked just like *you!*

WALTER. I just wondered if you've made up your mind and
everything.

BENEATHA. (*Gaining in sharpness and impatience.*) And
what did I answer yesterday—and the day before that, and
the day before that?

RUTH. (*Trying to talk over this argument and being stead-*
fastly ignored.) Don't be nasty, Bennie.

WALTER. (*Defensively.*) I'm interested in you. There ain't
too many girls I know who decide—

WALTER and BENEATHA. (*In unison.*) —"TO BE A DOC-
TOR." (*Silence.*)

BENEATHA. Give up, Walter. The insurance money belongs
to Mama. It's hers. Not ours. H.E.R.S.—*hers.*

WALTER. Oh, but she can always take a few thousand
dollars and help you through medical school, can't she!

BENEATHA. (*With fury, desperate to finally end this.*) What do you want from me, Brother—that I quit college or just drop dead, WHICH!?

WALTER. I don't want nothing from you except that maybe you stop acting holy 'round here! Oh, now, it ain't like anybody expects you to get down on your knees and say, thank you, Brother; thank you, Ruth and Mama, for working in somebody's kitchen to help put the clothes on your back—

BENEATHA. Well, I *do*—all right? (*Dropping to her knees in prayer.*) Thank you. Thank everybody. And forgive me for ever wanting to be anything at all! (*Pursuing him on her knees across the floor.*) Forgive me! Forgive me! Forgive me!

WALTER. (*Escaping D. L. by rocker.*) Get out of my face. If you so crazy 'bout messing 'round with sick people, why don't you go out and be a nurse like other women? (*Looking out.*) Or just get married and shut up!

BENEATHA. (*After him again, crossing D. R. of table.*) Well— you finally got it said. It took you three years, but you finally got it said. Listen, Walter, picking on me is not going to make Mama invest in any liquor store— (*Turning away to end it. Then, underbreath.*) and I for one say, God Bless Mama for that!

WALTER. (*To* RUTH, *shocked.*) See—did you hear? Did you hear! (*Crosses to sofa to get chauffeur's cap and jacket.*)

RUTH. Honey, will you go to work.

WALTER. Ain't nobody ever gonna understand me in this house! (*He starts for the door.*)

BENEATHA. (*A beat. As he is halfway out the door—drily.*) Because you're a nut.

WALTER. (*To God—who alone in this room understands him.*) We are one group of men *tied* to a race of women with *small* minds! (*He stalks out.* BENEATHA *heads for the bathroom.*)

RUTH. Bennie, why you always got to be pickin' on your brother?

BENEATHA. (*Standing outside the unseen bathroom door.*) Mrs. Johnson, will you come out of there, please! (*Bangs on the door. Then cheerfully.*) YOUR APARTMENT'S ON FIRE!! (*As she stands outside, squirming in urgent need to relieve herself,* WALTER ⌐eenters *and* BENEATHA *freezes as the focus shifts to him. He stands sheepishly in the doorway, looking from* RUTH *to the floor.*)

WALTER. I—uh— (*He fumbles with his cap, starts to speak, hesitates, flounders helplessly, and finally throws up his arms.*) I need some money for carfare.

RUTH. (*A beat. She turns away, out front, suppressing a smile. Sweetly, twisting the knife, as she reaches into her pocket.*) Fifty cents? (*Tosses him "the coin."*) Here. (*He reaches up to catch it in midair—to the "TING" OF A TRIANGLE.*) Take a taxi! (*He grins begrudgingly. Music Cue V [Score #4]:* RUTH *exits* L., *and* WALTER, R.—*through the* SOUTHSIDERS *who surge on, from all directions. Several of them quickly move table and chairs* U. L. *below sofa and remove rocker off* L.)

ACT ONE

SCENE 2

Chicago—the Southside and the Loop. Morning rush-hour: a montage.

As the backdrop turns vivid red and orange, the stage explodes with frenzied SOUTHSIDERS *"runnin' to meet the man."*

A CROWD *of 8 rush on from* D. R. *to line up, pushing and elbowing for air at a changebooth and turnstile,* D. C., *where they await a bus. Others crowd into a subway car,* U. C., *in what a moment ago was the bedroom,* SOME *seated on the bed, the* REST *clutching straphangers.*

The MUSIC is staccato and driving, and the babel of their voices a rising, jumbled cry of frustration.

SOUTHSIDERS. (*Ad-libbing as they come, with lines like the following.*)
Hey, man, does this bus stop at 63rd and Cottage?
Two, please.
You got the time? What time is it?
I hear they hiring at the yards. You hear that?
Miss, you forgot your change.
Move it along, buster.
You ain't the only one in line.

Hey, man, I heard your old lady's selling combat boots on the avenue.

Did you see her, man? Might of been *your* mama.

Quit shovin', okay?

Sorry.

SONG: "RUNNIN' TO MEET THE MAN"

(SUBWAY RIDERS *become dancing straphangers on the moving, swerving vehicle, as red and green traffic lights flash on and off from overhead, while the* BUS QUEUE *look left on the beats in search of the bus.*)

RUNNIN' TO MEET THE MAN,

RUNNIN' TO MEET THE MAN,

RUNNIN' AN' RACIN', NO TIME FOR PACIN',

RUNNIN' TO MEET THE MAN.

(QUEUE *crowds into the bus, side by side,* D. L.)

Hey, man, what stop is this?

Please get outta the way.

Say, mister, would you get your newspaper out of my face.

Sorry.

Lady, those are my feet you're standing on.

Hey, mama—

Do I look like your mama to you?

My station! I missed my station!

Move your ass, please!

God is lo-ove!

(WALTER *rushes in from* D. R., *bangs on the bus door, and squeezes his way in through the people.*)

WALTER.

JAMMED UP PEOPLE

SHUFFLIN' ALONG LIKE AN ARMY OF ANTS,

DOIN' THE SAME OLD DANCE.

SOUTHSIDERS.

RUNNIN' TO MEET THE MAN,

RUNNIN' TO MEET THE MAN,

OUT OF THE TROUBLE, OUT OF THE FIRE,

INTO THE FRYIN' PAN!

(*Vehicles jolt to a halt and all break out of the bus and subway to become pedestrians rushing to work.* WALTER, D. C., *tries to break through toward* U. C. *but finds himself blocked at every turn.*)

WALTER.
NO WAY I'M EVER GONNA BE A MAN OF MEANS
SWIMMIN' WITH SARDINES.

SOUTHSIDERS.
RUNNIN' TO MEET THE MAN.
RUNNIN' TO MEET THE MAN.
RUNNIN'S A HABIT, JUST LIKE A RABBIT,
END UP WHERE YOU BEGAN.

WALTER. (*He has at last made it to the bedroom,* U. C.)
DON'T BE LATE!
HE CAN'T WAIT!
HE'S GOT TO KNOW YOU'RE THERE
SO HE CAN OPERATE.

(*All are now spread across the* U. *and* D. *areas, running and
rushing* in place *to get to work.* WALTER, *in a follow spot, runs
through them to* R., *then* D. R., *and upstairs to balcony* C.)

SOUTHSIDERS.
RUNNIN', RACIN', JUMPIN', CHASIN',
RUNNIN' TO MEET THE MAN.
SKIPPIN' HOPPIN', THERE'S NO STOPPIN' . . .
CAUGHT UP IN HIS NOWHERE PLAN.

(*Still in place, they now speed up their movements while*
WALTER *looks down from balcony* C.)

WALTER.	SOUTHSIDERS.
DON'T BE LATE! HE CAN'T WAIT!	RUNNIN', RACIN', JUMPIN', CHASIN',
HE'S GOT TO KNOW YOU'RE THERE	RUNNIN' TO MEET THE MAN.
SO HE CAN OPERATE.	SKIPPIN', HOPPIN', THERE'S NO STOPPIN' . . .
DON'T BE LATE! HE CAN'T WAIT—	CAUGHT UP IN HIS NOWHERE PLAN.

(*He runs downstairs and hops onto the bed,* U. C., *which becomes his boss's car and* WALTER *the chauffeur, as all break
into work patterns: the* WOMEN *scrubbing the floor on their
knees, hanging clothes (from the balcony), typing, waiting
tables, doing household chores, etc., the* MEN *digging ditches,
toting bundles, washing windows (on the balcony), shining
shoes, pushing broom, operating a steam-pressing machine,
and hanging the clothes on a rack, etc. The song picks up its
frenzied tempo.*)

WALTER.
JAMMED UP! FOULED UP!
NOWHERE PEOPLE, NOWHERE FACES,
RUNNIN' AND RACIN' TO NOWHERE PLACES.
YOU RIDE ON BUSSES, YOU PUSH AND YOU
     SQUEEZE
JUST TO GET TO WORK, BE DOWN ON YOUR
     KNEES.
JAMMED UP! FOULED UP!
NOWHERE PEOPLE, NOWHERE FACES,
RUNNIN' AND RACIN' TO NOWHERE PLACES.
(*All start to run in place, in unison and slow motion, as* WALTER *starts driving and the amplified off-stage* VOICE OF HIS BOSS *issues the day's itinerary.*)

MR. ARNOLD. (O. S., *cheerfully at ease.*) Good morning, Walter. It's a lovely day. First stop, Calumet Steel.

WALTER. Yes, sir.

MR. ARNOLD. Twelve noon, the Stockyards. 2:15, pick me up at the Athletic Club.

WALTER. Yes, sir. (*Screech of brakes and horns from the orchestra.* WALTER *swerves at the wheel.*)

MR. ARNOLD. Walter, you missed that taxi by inches! Do you want to get me killed?

WALTER. (*Pungently and unmistakably.*) Yes, sir. (*He jams on the brakes, gets out and starts* D. C.)

MR. ARNOLD. What's that? Walter, you're not even listening to me! Walter, where are you going?

WALTER. I'll just be a minute, sir. (*He crosses through the throngs into a phone booth,* D. C., *dials his call—as the* ENSEMBLE *move into positions across the stage behind him, runnin' to meet the man again.*)

SOUTHSIDERS.
RUNNIN' RUNNIN' RUNNIN' RUNNIN' RUNNIN'
     RUNNIN'
RUNNIN' RUNNIN' RUNNIN' RUNNIN' RUNNIN'
     RUNNIN'

WALTER. (*With great excitement as the* SOUTHSIDERS *suddenly halt to a music beat.*) Hello, Willie? (*MUSIC up. They start up, then halt again.*) I got the money! (*They start, then halt again. Triumphantly.*) We gotta talk BUSINESS!! (*They start, then freeze, looking at their watches.*) TONIGHT! (*Music out. He hangs up the phone.* BLACKOUT. SOUTH-

SIDERS *rush off in all directions. Music Cue VI [Score #5]:*
As blue lights bathe the stage—these will be used for a number
of scene transitions—two remaining COUPLES *reset tables and*
chairs and exit chatting, U. R. *and* D. L., *with a final wave to*
each other.)

ACT ONE

SCENE 3

The apartment. Late afternoon.

As MAMA's *theme drifts gently up from the woodwinds, she*
   enters from D. R., *and unlocks the door. The lights come*
   up within. She looks about, takes off hat, coat and purse,
   and drops them on the sofa, while speaking.

MAMA. Lord, seem like them steps is getting longer and
longer. Time was when I could do a full day's work and not
feel a thing, and here I can barely lift these old bones. Just
look at you— (*Crossing down to the window to talk to her*
plant.) you look more wore out than I do. Poor little no 'count
scraggly thing! (*Picks it up. Confidentially, with a glint.*)
How'd you like a garden? Shoot! I bet *you* don't even know
what a garden is! Well, just you wait.

SONG: "A WHOLE LOTTA SUNLIGHT"

HOLD ON, LITTLE SPROUT,
SITTIN' THERE REACHING OUT,
AIN'T NO TIME TO FALL.
TIME TO STAND UP TALL!
HOLD ON, LITTLE SPROUT,
DON'T BE LETTING GO.
(*Sits in the rocker with the plant in her lap.*)
WON'T BE LONG 'FORE YOU STARTS TO GROW.

THERE'LL BE A WHOLE LOTTA SUNLIGHT,
NOTHIN' BUT BLUE IN THE SKIES,
BRIGHT YELLOW BLOSSOMS CATCHING
   BUTTERFLIES.

AND WHEN THE LEAVES ARE LULLABYING IN
    YOUR EAR . . .
WON'T NEED TO OPEN UP YOUR EYES
TO KNOW THE TIME OF YEAR.

TIME TO GET OUT IN THE MORNING.
TIME TO BATHE IN THE GLOW.
AND WHEN THAT LAZY OL' SUN SETS
JUST YOU LET IT GO.
NO NEED TO SIT AROUND REMEMB'RING
HOW IT USED TO BE.
THERE'LL BE A WHOLE LOTTA SUNLIGHT
SHINING FOR YOU AND ME.

Well, you see now, there's this nice little house, and it's got yellow shutters on the windows and ain't many cars comin' through the street—be real safe for Travis. Don't you know, they calls it a "dead end" street! Now ain't that a funny name for a street where some folks lives *begin! (Shaking her head with wonder, she stands and reaches out as if to embrace all the sunlight in the room.)*

TIME TO GET OUT IN THE MORNING.
(Crossing to the sink.)
TIME TO BATHE IN THE GLOW.
(Waters the plant.)
AND WHEN THAT LAZY OL' SUN SETS
JUST YOU LET IT GO.
(Crossing back to the window.)
NO NEED TO SIT AROUND REMEMB'RING
HOW IT USED TO BE.
THERE'LL BE A WHOLE LOTTA SUNLIGHT
SHINING FOR YOU AND ME.
(Puts the plant back in place and opens the curtains.)
WON'T BE LONG 'FORE YOU STARTS TO GROW.
(Stands looking wistfully out for a moment as Music *continues to end, then crosses toward the refrigerator—as* RUTH *enters, exhausted from the day's work. At the sight of* MAMA, *she brightens.)*

    RUTH. Evening, Lena.
    MAMA. Evening, child.
    RUTH. *(Crosses to drop her purse on the sofa, then back to table.)* Bless God this day is over! *(She sinks into a chair, table R., and kicks off her shoes.)*

MAMA. Tired?

RUTH. You know it! (*Extending her feet with relief and flexing her toes.*)

MAMA. Well, I got a nice cool drink for you. (*Gets a pitcher out of the refrigerator and a glass from the cupboard.*) Been one of them days?

RUTH. (*Rubbing her feet.*) Uh huh. (MAMA *pours the drink and* RUTH *takes it gratefully, then subtly changes the subject.*) Mama, I—been thinkin' about it all day—

MAMA. (*Anticipating and pleased.*) —the check?

RUTH. (*Startled, but glad it's out in the open.*) The check.

MAMA. Ten thousand dollars . . .

RUTH. Sure is wonderful. What you aim to do with it?

MAMA. (*Crossing behind* RUTH *to draw the younger woman's head back against her and soothe her temples.*) Oh, I ain't rightly decided yet, child. 'Cept one thing's for sure: the money for Beneatha's medical schoolin' gets put away first. Ain't nothin' gonna touch that part. (MAMA *hesitates—and delicately puts her new idea forth, massaging* RUTH's *shoulders and alert for her reaction.*) And then I kinda been thinkin', maybe we could meet the notes on a little ol' two-story somewhere if we use part of the money for a down payment and everybody just kind of pitch in . . .

RUTH. (*Matter-of-fact and with no hesitation.*) Well, Lord knows, we put enough rent into this here rat-trap.

MAMA. (MAMA *is momentarily stunned and then looks around, sighs and agrees.*) Rat-trap?—yes, I guess that's all it is, all right. (*Smiles as she thinks back to better days, taking a few steps* D. L. *of table.*) But I remember just as well the day me and Big Walter moved in here. That was a long time ago—

RUTH. He sure was a fine man, Mr. Younger.

MAMA. (*Laughing.*) God knows there was plenty wrong with Big Walter!— Hard-headed. Mean. Kinda wild with the women— (*She turns serious.*) But he sure loved his children. Always wanted them to *have* something . . . *be* something. He used to say—remember, Ruth— (*Standing straight and tall, head thrown back, looking off in re-creation of the robust voice, the poetry and dignity of the man.*) "Seem like God didn't see fit to give the black man nothing but dreams—but He did give us *children* to make them dreams seem worthwhile!" (*She becomes herself again, smiling.*) He could talk like that, don't you know.

RUTH. (*Agreeing—and at the same time trying to turn the conversation around.*) Yes, Walter Lee's a lot like Big Walter —he got *his* dream too . . .

MAMA. (*Shaking her head, refusing to consider the thought.*) Different, Ruth. Different dreams today.

RUTH. (*Gently trying to persuade her.*) No. It's the same dream, Lena.

MAMA. (*Firmly, crossing* D. *to rocker.*) *No.* In my time we was worried about not being lynched and getting to the North and how to stay alive and still have a pinch of dignity, too . . . but today . . . (*Shrugs.*)

RUTH. Today they's just got different ways of getting there. Now Walter Lee, he—

MAMA. (*Cutting her off as she sits in the rocker.*) Now we ain't no business people, Ruth.

RUTH. (*Rising with urgency.*) It ain't just that store or the money, Lena. He *needs* something. (*Going to her.*) I mean something I can't give him no more. He needs this chance.

MAMA. But *liquor,* honey . . .

RUTH. (*Comically, trying to lighten the mood as she crosses back to her chair but does not sit.*) Well, like Walter Lee say —people gonna always be drinkin' themselves some liquor . . .

MAMA. (*With finality.*) Well, whether they drinks it or not ain't none of my business. But whether I sells it to 'em *is—* (*The Irresistible Force and Immovable Object in one.*) and I do not want that on my ledger this late in life! (*A beat.* BENEATHA *enters* D. R.)

RUTH. (*Urgently.*) But, mama, it means so much to him. He talks about it day and night— (*She is interrupted by* BENEATHA'S *cheerful entrance.*)

BENEATHA. Hi, y'all. (*She bounces in and across* L., *drops her books on the sofa and immediately starts back out.*) 'Bye, y'all.

MAMA. Where you goin', Bennie? You just come in here!

BENEATHA. (*At the door. With enthusiasm.*) I start my conga drum lessons today. (MAMA *and* RUTH *look up with the same expression.*)

MAMA. You *what* kinda lessons?

BENEATHA. Conga drum. (*Starts playing an imaginary drum —over and about* RUTH *and across the room to* MAMA.)

RUTH. Oh Father, here we go again!

MAMA. (*Bewildered.*) What makes you take it in your head to try to learn to play . . . What?

BENEATHA. The conga drums! (*A final flourish on the conga, practically in* MAMA's *lap.*) I just want to. That's all. (*Pecks* MAMA *on the cheek and crosses to the sink for a glass of water, rinsing before drinking.*)

MAMA. (*Shaking her head with concern.*) Lord, child, you don't know what to do with yourself, do you? How long before you get tired of this now like you got tired of that world government group you just joined? And what was it before that?

RUTH. (*Amused.*) Weaving.

MAMA. And before that? (*Trying to remember.*) Uh . . . that thing about Aunt Vivian?

BENEATHA. (*Lowering the glass. Aloof—like a teacher to slow pupil.*) "Anti-vivisection."

MAMA. (*Nodding. Recalling.*) That's right! And what's it gonna be next?!

RUTH. Who knows! Probably belly dancing. (*Half-rising, she demonstrates.*)

MAMA. (*Genuinely concerned.*) Why you got to flit so from one thing to another, baby?

BENEATHA. (*Flustered, defensive.*) I don't flit. I— (*Patiently.*) I experiment with different forms of expression.

MAMA. (*A beat. She absorbs this, very interested, clears her throat, then.*) What is it you want to express?

BENEATHA. (*She flounders helplessly—and explodes.*) ME!! (RUTH *and* MAMA *look at each other—and simultaneously burst into raucous laughter.* BENEATHA *heads for the door.*)

RUTH. (*Crossing* D. *to* MAMA.) Never mind, Lena. She'll stop flitting when the right man comes along.

BENEATHA. (*Turning back, indignant.*) "Right man"!? Listen, men are all right to go out with and stuff—

RUTH. (*For sheer devilment. Crossing to* BENEATHA, U. S. *of table.*) What does "and stuff" mean?

MAMA. (*Still laughing.*) Stop pickin' on her now, Ruth. (*Tickled anew,* MAMA *turns* D. S. *convulsed, while* BENEATHA *flaunts her momentary "vindication" at* RUTH *and heads for the door. She is halfway out the door when* MAMA, *suddenly seized by suspicion, in mid-laugh and without warning, bellows fiercely:*) WHAT *DOES* IT MEAN? (*Turns to face her daughter.*)

BENEATHA. (*Wearily.*) I just mean that men are the last thing on my mind right now.

RUTH. (*Still playing with her.*) What's the *first*, Bennie?

BENEATHA. (*No longer amused.*) Oh God!

MAMA. (*Shocked at her language.*) Beneatha! I won't have you taking the Lord's name in vain . . .

RUTH. (*Still playing, trying to lighten things.*) Come on, what's the first, Bennie?

BENEATHA. (*In deadly earnest. Advancing on* RUTH.) Being a Doctor—and everyone around here better understand that!

MAMA. (*Kindly, not doubting it in the least.*) 'Course you gonna be a doctor, honey, God willing.

BENEATHA. (*Irritated.*) God hasn't got a thing to do with it.

MAMA. Beneatha, that just wasn't necessary.

BENEATHA. Well, neither is God.

MAMA. (*Shocked.*) Beneatha!

RUTH. Fresh, just fresh as salt, this girl!

BENEATHA. Oh, for Chrissakes, Ruth!

MAMA. (*Warning her.*) If you take the Lord's name just one more time . . .

BENEATHA. (*Crossing below table toward* MAMA.) Why! Why can't I say what I want around here like everybody else?

MAMA. (*A gentle explanation.*) 'Cause it don't sound nice for a young girl . . .

BENEATHA. Mama, you don't understand. (*Kneels beside her to patiently explain.*) It's all a matter of ideas, and God is just one idea I don't accept.

MAMA. Beneatha!

BENEATHA. Now I'm not going to go out and be immoral on account of it. (*Carried away by her own eloquence, she rises and drifts* D. C., *almost forgetting where she is and to whom she is speaking, in pursuit of a larger vision.*) It's just that I'm tired of *Him* getting the credit for all the things the human race achieves through its own stubborn effort! There simply is no blasted God! There is only Man— (*Climactically, savoring each word.*) —and it is *he* who makes miracles! (*She stands looking out, possessed by the thought, as* MAMA *rises and starts toward her.* BENEATHA *turns at last—and* MAMA *slaps her powerfully across the face. In the silence that follows the daughter averts—but does not drop—her eyes, as the mother stands tall before her.*)

MAMA. Now—you say after me: In my mother's house there is still God. (*Pause—in spite of everything,* BENEATHA *can-*

not bring herself to say the words. MAMA *takes her face by the chin and turns it toward her own. With inexorable precision.*) In my mother's house there is still God.

BENEATHA. (*Several beats, then very softly—eyes level, unyielding, but not to provoke.*) In my mother's house there is still God.

MAMA. (*Firmly.*) There's just some ideas we ain't gonna have in this house. Not as long as I'm the head of this family.

BENEATHA. (*Almost inaudibly.*) Yes, ma'am. (MAMA *turns away and crosses to her rocker and sits, while* BENEATHA *rushes for the door.*)

RUTH. (*Following* BENEATHA.) Bennie! (BENEATHA *runs off.* RUTH *shakes her head, takes a step toward* MAMA, *thinks better of it, picks up things on the sofa, and exits quickly,* L.)

MAMA. (*Greatly agitated, fighting for composure, her fist rising and falling on the arm of the rocker.*) My children! One done almost lost his mind thinkin' 'bout money . . . and the other— (*She lifts her hand helplessly, lets it fall, and starts to rock—then sits forward again as the lights close in.*) Yeah, they my children . . . but how different we done become! (*She resumes rocking as the lights—*)

DIMOUT

(Music Cue VII [Score #6].)

ACT ONE

SCENE 4

A Southside bar. That night.

Against the slate blue of night, the stage now crystallizes into a neighborhood bistro bathed in reds and the neon of a sign flickering on and off outside. The MUSIC is loud and groovy, the atmosphere swinging, funky, and the place teems with SOUTHSIDERS *of all ages gettin' down and having fun after the long day's work.* MAN *removes* MAMA's *rocker and plant off* L. *A* WAITER *serves drinks, a* COUPLE *slowdrags, others mill around in the mysterious shadows of the bar,* U. C., *or perch laughing or smooching*

on the levels, U. L., *while the young* DUDES *and* CHICKS
boogie and jitterbug around a table, D. L.

In a spotlight atop the table, ALTHEA *the proprietress, a
sizzling, well turned-out soul sister, is singing and fingerpopping, while* WALTER LEE *and* BOBO JONES, *standing on
chairs to her* L. *and* R. *respectively, are singing and jiving
right along with her.* BOBO, *in a square, obviously not too
prosperous suit, is an older, somewhat defeated man—but
at the moment you cannot tell it as, in high jubilation,
the three bounce the song back and forth between them
and the* DANCERS *respond with exuberance.*

SONG: "BOOZE"*

ALTHEA,WALTER, BOBO.
BOOZE, FAITHFUL BOOZE,
ALTHEA.
ONLY BOOZE CAN CHASE THE BLUES!
WALTER.
LET'S HAVE ANOTHER . . .
SOMEONE'S GONNA BUY.
BOBO.
LET'S HAVE ANOTHER,
HAVE ANOTHER *SEEDLESS* RYE.
(MAN *enters, opens bar and locks it into position.*)
BOBO and WALTER.
LET'S HAVE ANOTHER.
ONE MORE ALL AROUND!
BOBO. (*Lifting his glass.*)
WHAT A LOVELY WAY TO DROWN!
ALTHEA.
BOOZE, STRONGER BOOZE,
REALLY CAN—
(*With a sexy bellyroll for the double entendre.*)
—LIGHT YOUR FUSE!
WALTER.
LET'S HAVE ANOTHER.
KEEP IT COMIN', PLEASE!
BOBO.
LET'S HAVE ANOTHER,
FIND ANOTHER JUG TO SQUEEZE.

*NOTE TO CONDUCTOR: Tempo of this song should swing—but not
so fast as to kill the puns and *double entendre* of the lyrics.

WALTER.
DON'T CALL MY MOTHER.
PUT IT ON THE TAB—
BOBO. (*Ripping out his liver.*)
AND SEND MY LIVER TO THE LAB!
ALTHEA.
BOOZE, STEADY BOOZE,
POURS ON THE HAPPY NEWS!
WALTER.
A CHUG-A-LUG A PONY WINE.
BOBO.
A JUG OF GIN'LL DO ME FINE.
WALTER.
ANOTHER BLAST! ANOTHER SHOT!
BOBO.
I'M DRINKIN' ANYTHING YOU GOT!
WALTER.
MAKE IT SCOTCH!
BOBO.
MAKE IT RYE!
WALTER.
MAKE IT WET!
BOBO.
MAKE IT DRY!
WALTER.
STRAIGHT UP!
BOBO.
ON ICE!
WALTER.
THAT'S COOL!
BOBO.
THAT'S NICE!
WALTER.
HIGHBALL!
BOBO.
LOW BALL!
ALTHEA, WALTER, BOBO and ENSEMBLE.
WE LOVE IT ALL!
ALTHEA.
WE LOVE IT ALL!
SWEETER THAN HONEY DEWS!

(*The MUSIC continues under as a light picks up* WILLIE
HARRIS, *dapper and smoothly assured, on the balcony* U. C. R.)

WILLIE. Hey Bobo! Big Willie's here. On the scene. (*Holding up a contract in one hand.*) I got the deal. Get up—
(*With emphasis, fingering the anticipated cash between thumb
and forefingers.*) the *green!*

BOBO. Willie! The man of the hour! (BOBO *helps* ALTHEA
off the table and they start R. *as* WILLIE *sweeps briskly down
onto the club dance floor. Simultaneously* DANCERS *move table
and chairs* U. L. *During this:*)

WALTER. Hey, Willie, we been waitin' for you. You two
drinks late!

WILLIE. I'll catch up.

BOBO. (*Excited, a little man not used to triumphs.*) He's
got the papers, Walter Lee, he's got the papers—

WALTER. I know, Bobo, I know.

BOBO. (*As* WILLIE *approaches,* D. R.) Got the papers, Willie?

WILLIE. (*Waving them.*) In my fist! Three-way partners
. . . Willie Harris—the party of the first part . . . (*Flips*
ALTHEA *neatly about and signs with a flourish on her bosom.*)
Bobo Jones—the party of the second part . . . (*Hands the
papers to* BOBO *who also signs—at first on her rump, then,
corrected by a look, on her back.*) And Walter Lee Younger—
(*Starts to hand the papers to* WALTER, *at* C., *but stops.*) You
got your share, right, Walter Lee?

WALTER. Oh sure, Willie . . . practically in my hands right
now . . . (*He reaches for the papers but comes up with air—
as* WILLIE *pulls them back and crosses away,* R.)

WILLIE. Practically? (*Very cool, studying his cuffs.*) What
you mean, "practically"?

WALTER. I mean . . . I'll have it in a day or so.

WILLIE. (*With ultra reserve.*) "Day or so"? (*Studying his
fingernails.*) I—ah—know how long a day is . . . how long is
"so"?

WALTER. (*Too quickly, as he sees it all slipping away.*) I'll
have it, Willie. I'll have it.

WILLIE. You know, Walter Lee—ain't nobody standin' over
you with no baseball bat makin' you come in on this deal.
Are you out or are you in, man?

BOBO. Yeah . . . is you in or is you out?

WALTER. I'm in, Willie . . . I'm in . . . (Start of SAFETY
VAMP.)

BOBO. He's in, Willie, he's in.

WILLIE. Then put your Walter Lee right here . . . (*Crossing c., hands him pen and papers.*)

WALTER. Sure, Willie . . . (*Starts to sign, then suddenly hesitates.*) Just one thing.

WILLIE. I'm listenin'.

WALTER. You sure that's the right— (*Stalling for time and finally coming up with an irrelevancy.*) —location for a liquor store?

BOBO. (*To* WILLIE.) Yeah, man, the right location . . .

WILLIE. (*A beat, looks from one to the other, then.*) Man! You show me the *WRONG* location for a liquor store! (WILLIE *and* BOBO *exchange skin.* WALTER *signs.*) Gentlemen, when you're selling booze— (*Punching out each word in time to the beat of the music.*) you just can't lose! (End of SAFETY VAMP. ENSEMBLE *breaks into a frenzied finish to the dance.*)

WALTER, WILLIE, BOBO and ALTHEA.
LET'S HAVE ANOTHER,
REALLY POUR IT ON!
LET'S HAVE ANOTHER
'FORE ANOTHER SWALLOW'S GONE.

WALTER, WILLIE and BOBO.
BROTHER TO BROTHER—
HOW WE GONNA LOSE?

ALL.
FAITHFUL BOOZE, STEADY BOOZE,
ALWAYS RIGHT AND READY BOOZE!

WALTER.
ONLY BOOZE CAN CHASE THE BLUES!

ALL.
—CAN CHASE THE BLUES!

(ALL *freeze—and abruptly*—Music Cue VIII [Score #6A] —*dancers explode all over the stage in a second dance finale, as* WALTER, WILLIE *and* BOBO *leap onto the bar and nearby levels and sing a trumpet trio.*)

WALTER, WILLIE and BOBO.
DOO WAH, DOO WAH, DOO WAH
DOO WAH, DOO WAH, DOO WAH
DOO WAH, DOO WAH, DOO WAH
DOO WAH, DOO WAH, DOO WAH, DOO WAH

(*At the climax, the* THREE PARTNERS *jump to the ground and complete an elaborate, three-way ritual handshake that closes the deal as the* SOUTHSIDERS *leap and freeze in a final jitter-bug pose.* Cut off. End of Music. *As the lights dim out stage* L.—Music Cue VIIIA [Score #6A, Bar 70]. WALTER, WILLIE, BOB *and* ALTHEA *exit bopping up the stairs,* D. R., *and* ALL *dance off—except for* TWO BOPPERS *who do a few final turns at* R. *before leaving—as* MAMA, BENEATHA *(carrying rocker),* RUTH, *and* TRAVIS *(bringing plant), from* L., *stride briskly on and into—)*

ACT ONE

SCENE 5

The apartment. Next morning.

RUTH, TRAVIS, MAMA, BENEATHA, *enter from* L. *and take positions indicated.* When scene is set, Music Cut Off.

It is Saturday—housecleaning day. RUTH, *in slacks and one of* WALTER's *shirts, crosses into her room to make the bed.* TRAVIS *sits in a chair.* MAMA *chases him away and turns the chair up on the table to sweep. He sits in the other chair, she chases him again, and he goes to the bedroom door to talk to* RUTH. *All the while,* BENEATHA, *on her knees in jeans and shirt,* D. C., *is vigorously and absorbedly spraying cockroaches.*

TRAVIS. Mama, can I please go down? That cockroach stuff smells awful.

RUTH. O.K., Travis. But, honey, you stay right out front and keep a good lookout for the mailman. O.K.?

TRAVIS. *(Eyeing* BENEATHA *as she sprays.)* Today Grandma's check coming, huh?

RUTH. Yes. Today is the day, baby. (TRAVIS *starts for the door.)*

MAMA. Don't miss under the sink, Bennie. I seen a cock-roach yesterday marching out of there like Napoleon! (TRAVIS *halts in the door, eyes* BENEATHA *with a devilish glint, rubs his hands with anticipation and bops slowly behind her, lay-ing in the words.)*

TRAVIS. Why don't you leave them poor little cockroaches

alone, girl, they ain't bothering you none. (*Winds up, smacks her on the butt and immediately darts behind* MAMA.) Grandma! Grandma! (BENEATHA *chases after him with spray gun aimed.*)

MAMA. (*As they circle her.*) Now look out there, girl, you be spilling that stuff on the child! Now just look out there, girl! (*Arms outstretched, blocking* BENEATHA.)

TRAVIS. (*Standing safely in the doorway, with great bravado.*) Yeah, that's right there, girl— (*With a cocky, jive gesture and a flavorful flourish.*) Just look out! (*He exits as* BENEATHA *goes back to her spraying.*)

BENEATHA. Well, I can't imagine it would hurt him—it has *never* hurt the roaches! (*The PHONE RINGS and* BENEATHA *and* RUTH *make a mad dash for it,* D. L., *almost running over* MAMA. RUTH *gets it and* BENEATHA *starts* R.)

RUTH. (*Expecting it to be* WALTER LEE.) Yeah, honey! (*Disappointed—it isn't.*) Oh, yes. She's here. (*Holds out the receiver—*BENEATHA, *triumphant, crosses back and takes it.* RUTH *moves away and* MAMA *starts sweeping.*)

BENEATHA. (*With elaborate composure, voice modulated to perfection.*) Hello. (*Excited and surprised.*) Oh, hello! (*A beat.*) Of course I've missed you . . . in my way! (RUTH, *who has drifted back to listen, leans closer—*BENEATHA *pushes her away with a look, and* RUTH *exits* L.) This morning? No, housecleaning. (MAMA *sweeps closer to eavesdrop. Shifting phone to the other ear.*) No, Mama hates it if I let anyone come over when the house is like this.

MAMA. (*Directly into the telephone.*) That's right!

BENEATHA. (*Embarrassed, squeezes a little further* L. *to escape and* MAMA *goes back to sweeping,* C., *Then.*) Really!?! Well, if you're *that* close by . . . Oh, what the hell, come on over! Right. *Ciao.* (*Hangs up and immediately starts* R. *to get ready.*)

MAMA. (*Outraged.*) Who is that? Girl, you ain't got the pride you was born with! (*Stops her from walking through dustpile.*)

BENEATHA. (L. *of* MAMA, *pulling up her socks and generally checking appearance.*) Oh Mama, Asagai doesn't care how houses look—he's an intellectual. (*As if that explains it all.*)

MAMA. *Who?*

BENEATHA. Asagai. Joseph Ah-sah-guy. (*Says this slowly, teacher to pupil, and then finishes quickly.*) He's from Nigeria.

MAMA. (*Digests it, then.*) Oh, that's that little country that was founded by slaves way back . . . (*Pleased with her knowledge, she heads to the closet, D. L., for a dustpan.*)

BENEATHA. (Very *tolerantly.*) No, Mama, that's *L*iberia.

MAMA. (*Crossing back* C.) I don't think I never met no African before. (*Straining to think of another, she bends over to sweep up dust.*)

BENEATHA. Well, Mama, do me a favor and don't ask a whole lot of ignorant questions. Like do they wear clothes.

MAMA. (*Rising, insulted.*) Now, if you think we so ignorant 'round here, maybe you—

BENEATHA. (*Trying to smoothe it over.*) No, Mama, it's just that all anyone seems to know about Africa is Tarzan— (*Crossing toward U. C. bedroom.*)

MAMA. (*Indignant.*) Why should I know about Africa? (*Steering* BENEATHA *around dustpile.*)

BENEATHA. Why do you give money at church to the missionaries? (*Enters the bedroom.*)

MAMA. Well, that's to help save folks from heathenism.

BENEATHA. I'm afraid they need more salvation from the French, the English— (*Sticking her head back out of the bedroom.*) and the C.I.A.! (*The doorbell rings.* MAMA *picks up the trash and exits to her room, while* BENEATHA *frantically tries to fix herself up at the mirror and ends by spraying perfume behind her ears and under her arms—with her shirt still on. She dashes from the bedroom, catches herself and turns back for a final check in the mirror, sniffs under her arms and crosses to the door—where she stops to compose herself, and then* coolly *opens the door.* ASAGAI *stands there, composed, urbane, a striking young man in a dark suit, concealing a large package behind his back.*)

ASAGAI. Hello, Alaiyo.*

BENEATHA. (*Entranced.*) Hello . . . (*She hangs there paralyzed, at a loss for words. As he peers around her into the room, she comes back to reality.*) Well, come in . . . Have a seat, Asagai. (*The flustered hostess, she leads him to the couch, U. L., lifts chair from table and, forgetting herself, abruptly sits—leaving him still standing uncertainly. Amused, he looks at the front door, left open. She turns, sees, jumps up and closes it, and starts back.*) I'm very glad you're back! (*Then*

*Pronounced: Ah-lah-ee'yoh.

blurting abruptly, peremptorily, as if it's her due.) What'd you bring me? (*She sits. He sits.*)

ASAGAI. (*Smiling, as he sets the box before her on the table.*) What gives you the impression I brought you something? (BENEATHA *opens it—pulls out an African head wrap and scans the material underneath. Overcome by the beauty of the motif, she stands and moves* C., *holding the headpiece. Watching her, pleased, he crosses to her* R.) So . . . you like the robes? You must take excellent care of them—they are my sister's.

BENEATHA. (*Genuinely surprised that he would go to such trouble.*) You sent all the way home . . . for me?

ASAGAI. Not for *you!* For the *robes!* (*He says this dead pan, and then laughs.*)

BENEATHA. Asagai . . . can't you ever be serious about anything?

ASAGAI. (*Smiling.*) I am only teasing you because *you* are so very serious about *everything.* (*Gently, playfully.*) Do you remember when we first met at school? You came up to me and you said: (*Imitating her.*) "Mr. Asagai . . . I want very much to talk with you. About Africa. You see, Mr. Asagai, I am looking for . . . my *identity!*" (*He howls.*)

BENEATHA. (*Not laughing.*) Yes . . . I remember.

ASAGAI. (*Looking at her intently.*) Well, it is true, this is not so much the profile of a Hollywood Queen as perhaps . . . (*Lifting her chin with one hand and making a grand gesture.*) a Queen of the Nile. (*Drawing her towards him.*) Oh, yes, Alaiyo, I can indeed be quite serious about some things. (*As he leans in to kiss her,* MAMA *loudly clears her throat in the doorway* L.)

BENEATHA. (*Jumps and crosses to* MAMA *and brings her to* ASAGAI.) Oh . . . Mama . . . this is Joseph Asagai. Asagai, this is my Mama. (*The two stand facing each other at some distance: he* C., MAMA *to his* L.—BENEATHA *above and framed by the two of them.*)

MAMA. (*On her best behavior.*) How do you do? (*Shaking his hand vigorously.*)

ASAGAI. (*Total politeness to an elder.*) You must forgive me for coming at such an outrageous hour. (*He raises her hand to his lips.*)

MAMA. Well you are quite welcome I'm— (*He kisses her hand and releases it—she is stunned and for the moment the hand and next word linger in the air.*) sure! (BENEATHA *pulls the hand down; the conversation resumes.*) I do hope you understand that our house— (*Looking daggers at* BENEATHA.) don't *always* look like this! (BENEATHA *crosses* R. *behind* ASAGAI. *Charmingly.*) You must come again. I would like very much to hear all about— (*Fishing for the name—it doesn't come.*) your country. (*Proudly, a recital.*) I think it's so sad the way our poor American Negroes don't know nothing about Africa 'cept for Tarzan! And all that money they pour into these churches— (*Vigorously, shaking her finger for emphasis.*) when they should be—in there—helping you people drive out them French and English CPA's done taken away your land! (*Recitation completed—a superior look at her daughter.*)

ASAGAI. (*Floundering, with a look to* BENEATHA *for assistance.*) Yes . . . yes . . .

MAMA. (*Suddenly smiling, and relaxing.*) Well, I 'spec being so far away from your mama you better come 'round here and get yourself some decent home-cooked meals . . .

ASAGAI. Thank you. Thank you very much. (*Turning to* BENEATHA.) Is this agreeable with you also, Alaiyo? (*She nods.*)

MAMA. (*Immediately suspicious. To* BENEATHA.) What's that he call you?

ASAGAI. Oh . . . "Alaiyo." I hope you don't mind. It is what you would call a . . . nickname, I think. It is a Yoruba word. I am a Yoruba. (*He says the last with great pride.*)

MAMA. (*Feeling betrayed, looking daggers at* BENEATHA.) I thought you said he was from—

ASAGAI. (*Understanding.*) Nigeria is my country. Yoruba is my tribal origin.

MAMA. (*Looking at them both—hopelessly confused.*) Well . . . that's nice! (*Then, all charm again, as she prepares to leave.*) Do come again . . . Mr.— (*Hesitates, stuck.*)

ASAGAI. (*Gallantly.*) Ah-sah-guy. (*Gestures for her to try it.*)

MAMA. (*Starts to say it, can't, and continues.*) Yes . . . Do come again. (*He clicks his heels and bows crisply—she tosses her head triumphantly at* BENEATHA, *turns with a flourish and exits proudly* L.)

ASAGAI. Well, Alaiyo, I must go. (*Starts toward door.* Music Cue IX [Score #7]: SAFETY VAMP.)

BENEATHA. Oh, but Asagai, you still didn't say what— (*Mispronouncing it.*) Alaiyo means. (*Crossing coyly a little*

D. C.) For all I know you might be calling me "little idiot" or something.

ASAGAI. Well, let me see . . . (*Crossing L. with a look toward* MAMA's *room to check that this time they* are *alone.*) it is difficult when a thing changes languages. (*He takes out the African cloth and moves towards her.*)

SONG: "ALAIYO"

HOW TO SAY IT? HOW TO BEGIN?
ONE WHO SEARCHES WITHIN,
ALAIYO.
(*With a deft flourish he tosses the cloth out to its full length, and then drapes it about her in true Nigerian style during the stanza.*)
ONE WHO HUNGERS, SEEKING THE TRUE.
BREAD ALONE WILL NOT DO,
ALAIYO,
HOW TO TELL YOU?
PICTURE THE MOUNTAIN SO TALL,
RIVER SO WIDE.
ONE WHO DREAMS
OF REACHING THE OTHER SIDE,
ALAIYO.
BENEATHA.
SEEING YOUR WORLD TOUCHING ON MINE
WEAVES A WHOLE NEW DESIGN,
AL-A . . .
(*Hesitates.*)
ASAGAI.
ALAIYO.
BENEATHA.
ALAIYO.
ASAGAI.
SOMETHING STRONGER, SOMEHOW REBORN.
LIKE THE SUNLIGHT EACH DAWN,
ALAIYO.
BENEATHA.
ALAIYO.
ASAGAI.
HEARTBEATS TELL ME . . .
BEATING LIKE DRUMS OF MY HOME,

BENEATHA.
HEARTBEATS!
BENEATHA and ASAGAI.
CALLING MY NAME.
WE HAVE MADE OUR TWO DIFF'RENT WORLDS
    THE SAME,
ALAIYO.
ASAGAI.
EYES OF DARKNESS NEEDING THE LIGHT,
BENEATHA.
LIKE A BIRD NEEDING FLIGHT,
ALAIYO.
ASAGAI.
ALAIYO.
WAND'RING SOMEWHERE OVER A CLOUD,
FEELING STRONG, FEELING PROUD,
ALAIYO.
ASAGAI and BENEATHA.
ALL AROUND US, SEEING TOMORROW SO CLEAR,
ASAGAI.
SHINING SO TRUE.
BENEATHA.
CAN IT BE
BENEATHA and ASAGAI.
TOMORROW IS REALLY YOU?
BENEATHA.
ALAIYO.
ASAGAI.
ALAIYO.
BENEATHA.
ALAIYO.
ASAGAI.
ALAIYO.
BENEATHA.
ALAIYO.
BENEATHA and ASAGAI.
ALAIYO.
(*They stand, eyes locked, tremulous, as the* Music *ends. A
beat. As he is about to kiss her, she nervously breaks away.*)
    BENEATHA. (*A joke to cover.*) Well, I certainly *do* know
what "Alaiyo" means now!

ASAGAI. (*Very tentatively, afraid he'll be turned down.*) There is . . . an African Student Union reception tonight. I would very much like you to join me—wearing the robes. (*She hesitates; he speaks quickly to avoid a refusal, crossing to door.*) Do not decide now. I shall call you later. It might help you to find your—identity! (*As* TRAVIS *enters* D. R., ASAGAI *opens the front door. To himself, ecstatic.*) Op-pay-gay-day, oh-gbah-mu-shay! (*As he turns to go,* ASAGAI *sees* TRAVIS. *He strides forward, puts his hands on* TRAVIS' *shoulders and leapfrogs over the startled* BOY—*who, instinctively, whips off his jacket and puts up his dukes to defend himself.* ASAGAI *gives a lusty Tarzan yell, beats his chest and —as* TRAVIS *stands immobilized in shock—exits. The* BOY *turns and sees his* SISTER, *standing spellbound in the doorway.*)

TRAVIS. (*Looks her up and down thoroughly, then.*) Girl, you cracking up?

BENEATHA. Oh, shut up, boy! (BENEATHA *crosses back inside, followed by* TRAVIS. *She tremulously gathers up her robe and box as in a dream, and starts* D. *and then* L. *toward her room as* MAMA *returns.*)

MAMA. (*Stops at the sight of her.*) Where you goin', Bennie?

BENEATHA. (*Grandly.*) To become a Queen of the Nile! (*Assumes her Queen of the Nile stance and exits in a breathless blaze of glory—past* RUTH, *who enters from* L.)

RUTH. (*Having caught the tail end of this.*) Where did she say she was going?

MAMA. Far as I can make out—to Egypt. (*The doorbell rings and the* TWO WOMEN *freeze; in spite of all other distractions of the morning, this is what they have been waiting for.*)

RUTH and MAMA. (*Simultaneously.*) The mailman!

RUTH. (*Pushing him out the door.*) Travis, honey, get down them steps! (TRAVIS *runs out.*)

MAMA. (*Trying to get herself together.*) Well . . . well . . . I don't know what we getting so excited about. We knowed it was coming for months. (*Sits in her rocker.*)

RUTH. That's a whole lot different from having it come! (TRAVIS *bursts back in with the envelope in his hand . . . hands it to* RUTH . . . *who hands it to* MAMA.) Lord have mercy, I wish Walter Lee was here! Open it!

TRAVIS. (*Crosses to the* D. L. *side of the rocker.*) Open it, Grandma!

MAMA. Now you all be quiet, it's just a check. (*Trying to compose herself.*)

RUTH. Open it. (*Terribly excited.*)

MAMA. Now don't act silly! We ain't never been no people to act silly 'bout no money before . . .

RUTH. (*Swiftly, automatically.*) We ain't never *had* none before—*open it!*

MAMA. (*Finally tears open the letter and takes the check out and inspects it while the others peer on, and then holds it out for* TRAVIS *to look at.*) Travis . . . that the right number of zeros?

TRAVIS. (*Counts the zeros with his finger, then.*) That's the right number of zeros, Grandma. (*A beat.*) Grandma, you rich! (*He looks off calculatingly, then plants a kiss on her cheek, and then slips an arm 'round her shoulder.*)

MAMA. (*Suddenly on the verge of tears, hands it to* RUTH.) Put it away somewhere, Ruth. Ten thousand dollars they give you. (Music Cue X [Score #7A].)

TRAVIS. (*To his* MOTHER, *sincerely.*) What's the matter with Grandma?

RUTH. (*Pulls* TRAVIS *to the door and puts him out.*) Travis, honey, you go on out and play now, baby.

TRAVIS. Yes'm. (*He exits.* RUTH *goes into her room and sits on the* L. *edge of the bed, looking at the check, as the lights silhouette her and close on* MAMA.)

MAMA. Ten thousand dollars . . .

REPRISE: "A WHOLE LOTTA SUNLIGHT"

(*Choked up, fighting tears.*)
NO NEED TO SIT AROUND REMEMB'RING
HOW IT USED TO BE
. . . A WHOLE LOTTA SUNLIGHT
SHININ' . . .
(*She stops rocking and leans forward with determination.*)
No more rats, Ruth!

DIMOUT

(Music cut off *at last light.*)

ACT ONE
SCENE 6

That night, the apartment.

In the darkness, the sounds of a popular recording of the era, "SAME OLD COLOR SCHEME."* RUTH hums and sings along with the vocalist.

SINGER. (O. S., *recorded.*)
GREY SKIES, BLUE DREAMS
SAME OLD COLOR SCHEME
THERE'S NO MILK OR HONEY
THERE'S NO CREAM
GET HIGH—WHAT FOR?
THERE'S NO GOLDEN DOOR
THERE'S NO SILVER LINING
ANYMORE . . .

(As the lights come up, RUTH *comes out of bedroom, moves table into place, and positions two chairs behind rocker to balance her ironing board,* D. L. BENEATHA *sweeps on,* U. L., *in exaggerated imitation of Watusi. grace, clad in the African robes.* RUTH'S *mouth drops and she puts down the iron in fascination.)*

RUTH. And what are we up to tonight! (BENEATHA *sweeps grandly to the record player,* C., *with a mimed stack of records balanced on her head. She lifts the needle and loftily removes the record.)*

BENEATHA. Enough of this *assimilationist* junk! Let's put some real music on! (*She puts one of her records on—African drums and chants**—waits ceremoniously for the recording to start, and then abruptly whirls and leaps with an earsplitting shout toward* RUTH—*who almost drops the iron.)* OCOMO-GOSIAY!!‡ (BENEATHA *begins to dance—a melange of Pearl Primus, Dunham and Madam Butterfly.)*

RUTH. (*Drily—and very idiomatically.*) What kind of dance is that?

BENEATHA. (*Dancing vigorously.*) It's a folk dance.

RUTH. (*Pearl Bailey.*) What kind of folks do that, honey?

*This should be pre-recorded with the quality of an old 78; otherwise, substitute an actual record typical of the time. It should be clear that Ruth is casually singing along with the recorded voice, not delivering the song.
**In the original production, song by Michael Olatunji from his Columbia album "DRUMS OF PASSION" was used.
‡Mispronounced: Oh-coh-moh-*goo*'see-ay!

BENEATHA. It's from Nigeria. It's a dance of welcome.

RUTH. Who you welcoming?

BENEATHA. (*Going into a very sensual shimmy,* D.C.) The MEN! Back to the village.

RUTH. Where they been?

BENEATHA. (*Stopping suddenly.*) How should I know? (*Then, swept up into dance again.*) Out hunting, or something. Anyway, they coming back now! (*On these words,* WALTER *enters* U. R.—"*happy*" *drunk, tie loose, jacket slung over shoulder—and weaves his way unsteadily toward the door.*)

RUTH. Well, that's good. (WALTER *opens the door. As he turns to shut it,* BENEATHA *lets out a bloodcurdling whoop and charges at him. Scared out of his wits, he lunges into the wall with a shriek, clutching hat and jacket.*)

BENEATHA. Welcome back to the villAAAAAGE! (*As* BE-NEATHA *continues dancing* D. C., *he weaves unsteadily across the room, trying to blink or brush the scene away as though it were a large pink elephant. When he cannot, he turns to* RUTH.)

WALTER. Check come?

RUTH. Yeah, the check came. (*Now it is his turn:* WALTER *lets out a yell, kisses* RUTH *full on the lips, then turns to* BENEATHA *and flings up his arms as he, too, starts to dance.*)

WALTER. YEEEAAAH! (*Relishing each word.*) AND ETHIOPIA SHALL STRETCH FORTH HER ARMS AGAIN! (*He joins* BENEATHA, D. C.)

RUTH. (*Pithily, out front.*) Yes, Lord, and Africa sure is claiming her own tonight! (*Turning to him.*) Honey, I hope you ain't gone and done nothing—

WALTER. (*Dancing furiously.*) Shut up, woman! I'm digging them drums. Them drums *m-o-o-ove* me! (*He continues dancing, imitating his* SISTER.)

BENEATHA. OCOMOGOSIAY!

WALTER. OCOMOGOOOSIAY! In my heart of hearts— (*Thumping his chest.*) I am much warrior!

RUTH. (*Deadpan, out front.*) In your heart of hearts you are much drunkard! (*He stops short, gives her a look, reaches down for an imaginary spear, and suddenly hurls it at her, slipping backwards to the floor as he does.* RUTH *ducks—and resumes ironing.*)

BENEATHA. (*Dancing over him, worshipfully.*) Flaming Spear, OWIMOWEH!*

*Pronounced: oh-wee'moh-way

WALTER. (*Mimicking happily, drunkenly.*) Gaming Fear! O— (*To* BENEATHA *for help.*) O—*what?*

BENEATHA. *Owimoweh.*

WALTER. OWIMOWEH! Hot damn! (*He gets up off the floor and stalks the room, spearing "enemies" to* R. *and* L., *then hurls a final spear out over the audience.*) The LION— (*Spoken as if he himself were the sleeping mighty lion of the lore arisen at last.*) IS *WAKING!!* (Music Cue XI, 4/4 Rhythm [Score #9]. *He circles above the table and leaps upon it, falls back unable to negotiate it in his drunkenness, then mounts it again triumphantly. The lights shift magically, there is a shimmer of cymbal and drum, and suddenly an* AFRICAN WOMAN *appears as out of nowhere* U. L., *in gleaming bare splendor touched by feathers and beads, to rivet and hold him spellbound. As he stares and rubs his eyes, another appears* U. C., *then a third,* D. C., *each to bind him in turn; and they are followed at last by the* WARRIORS, *who enter with powerful movements from* U. L. *across the balustrade. As he drinks in the scene, the MUSIC has changed to the beat of live drums, but* BENEATHA— *not seeing what he sees—still dances to the old rhythm and* RUTH *continues ironing.* WALTER *raises his arms for attention. When he speaks it is poetically, in oracular tones, as a man transformed into a leader addressing "his" people, "his" tribe: a great chief or prophet, a vision of glory, on that day when the hour to march has come. The words—every image he paints—are all important here: now whispered, now shouted, incanted, caressed, impassioned, transcendent, but* always *plumbed to the marrow for the full symbolic weight, the beauty and power of the vision that commands him.*) Listen, my BLACK brothers!!

BENEATHA. (*Amazed, but enthusiastically going along with it.*) We hear you!

WALTER. Do you hear? Do you hear the waters rushing against the shores of our coastlands?

BENEATHA. OCOMOGOSIAY!

MALE SINGER. (O. S. *African warsong. A haunting call across the savannahs climaxing in a deep guttural roar—a primal shout tearing up from the gut.*) Sango oni bo de ola olola AAAGH!*

WALTER. Do you hear the screeching of the cocks in yonder

*Pronounced: Shahn-goh' aw-nee' baw day aw'lah aw-law'lah AAAGH

hills beyond where the chiefs meet in council for the coming
of the mighty war?

BENEATHA. OHURU!*

2ND MALE SINGER. (O. S.) Sango oni bo de ola olola AAGH!

WALTER. Do you hear the singing of the women—singing
the war songs of our fathers to the babies in the great houses?

BENEATHA. OCOMOGOSIAY!

FEMALE SINGER. (O. S.) Sango oni bo de ola olola AAAGH!

WALTER. Telling us the Day has come! (*As the chant and*
WALTER's *words build to a climax the* WARRIORS *surge down
from the balcony and leap to places opposite* WALTER.) The
Day of Greatness when we shall rise in our Glory—Rise my
Black Brothers—and Rule in Our Land! OH, do you hear
me—

BENEATHA. (*Underneath his last line.*) We hear you!

WALTER. —my *BLACK* BROTHERS! (WALTER *stamps his
foot on the table.* End 4/4, start of 6/8 Rhythm: *The stage
erupts with all the power, grace and excitement of African
dance, as more* DANCERS *enter, the Drums soar, the warsong
of the* SINGERS O. S. *resounds ever louder, and a few occasional
bird and animal jungle cries from one or two* DANCERS *punc-
tuate the spectacle. Ablaze with their spirit, picking up the
movements of first one, then another, he dances on the table
and then leaps down among them—while* BENEATHA, *too, joins
in the dance, this time imitating* WALTER—*who moves through
the* DANCERS *to find himself at last on the bedroom platform
U. C. At the climax, the* DANCERS *reach a frenzy, whirl and—on
a climactic sudden beat—*ALL *freeze and Drums stop. As the
applause subsides, he lifts his arms high.*) Oh, do you hear,
MY BLACK BROTHERS?! (*Crossing* D. *toward table.*)
Telling us to prepare for— (*Summoning all the power that is
in him.*) the GREATNESS— (*Clenches one fist triumphantly.*)
of the TIME!! (*Clenches the other. As the* Drums resume
and the DANCERS *exit as suddenly as they appeared, he leaps
to the table,* BENEATHA *slips onto it crouched between his
legs, and both emit a final extended whoop.*)

WALTER and BENEATHA. OWEEEE-MOWEHHHH! (*There
is a sudden loud knocking as* MRS. JOHNSON—*who has run
frantically on from* U. L. *during the exit—beats at the front
door.*)

MRS. JOHNSON. Lena! Lena! (*As* RUTH *lifts the arm from
the phonograph,* Music cut off, *and lights return to normal.*

*Pronounced: oh-hoo'roo

RUTH *opens the door and* MRS. JOHNSON *comes in, completely discombobulated.*) You all done gone c-c-c-crazy in here!?!

WALTER. (*Turning to her with arms outstretched worshipfully as are* BENEATHA's.) Daughter of Darkness! Rise up, great Queen of the ZULUS!! (*As the two reach towards her,* MRS. JOHNSON *backs away—and into* ASAGAI, *who has entered the open door from* U. R. *on* WALTER's *last words. She whirls, takes one look at his Yoruba regalia—he is dressed for the African reception—and comes apart.*)

MRS. JOHNSON. Lord have mercy, the Maus Maus!!! (*She flies out* U. *and off* L. BENEATHA *crosses to* ASAGAI *and takes his hand to introduce him to* WALTER *who is still on the table.*)

BENEATHA. Oh, Asagai, this is my brother, Walter Lee. (WALTER *extends his hand, but abruptly grabs his mouth in obvious need and dashes for the bathroom.* RUTH *and* BENEATHA *try to retain some composure.*) . . . And his wife, Ruth . . .

RUTH. (*Extending her hand, to salvage the moment.*) How d'you do. He's—had a little to drink . . . I don't know what her excuse is!

ASAGAI. (*As charming as ever.*) I have often been in the same position.

BENEATHA. (*Surprised to hear this.*) But, Asagai, you don't drink . . .

ASAGAI. You have never *seen* me drink, Alaiyo. That is not quite the same thing as not drinking. Goodnight, Mrs. Younger. (*As he speaks, he slips an African necklace about her neck, and they exit.* WALTER *reels in exuberantly,* L., *happy drunk, and surprises* RUTH, *sweeping her off her feet and over in a dramatic kiss. They both laugh. With a flourish he brings out his contract.*)

WALTER. See? (*Proudly pointing to the spot.*) All signed! (RUTH *says nothing.*) A full third partnership—me, Bobo, and Willie Harris! (*His excitement is growing.*) Now when is Mama coming home? (*To avoid answering or antagonizing him,* RUTH *starts to put away the ironing board and re-set the chairs.*) Check come? (*A beat.*) Yeah! You told me that already. (*Suddenly drawing her to him.*) Oh, baby, all I need now is the money!

RUTH. (*Very gently. On eggshells.*) Now, Walter, honey . . . between "needin'" the money and *gettin'* it . . . (*Her voice trails off, then another tack.*) You know your mama's got her own ideas . . . (*She starts* D. L. *for the things she has ironed.*)

WALTER. (*Abruptly resentful, sensing her reluctance.*) Mama? Or *you*, baby?

RUTH. (*She halts, then continues* D. L. *and picks up the ironing.*) All I'm saying is don't count on it, Walter, that's all. (*Crossing back to the table.*)

WALTER. And I'm saying I've known mama a lot longer than you have!

RUTH. But liquor, honey . . .

WALTER. WHY ISN'T EVER ENOUGH FOR ME TO TELL YOU I KNOW WHAT I'M DOING! (*She starts folding the ironing on the table compulsively and he slams his hands down in it to stop her.*) Now stop that! Mama's gonna come through. All right, baby? (*A beat. Tenaciously insisting, at the brink.*) All RIGHT?

RUTH. (*Lovingly—and protectively—touching his cheek.*) I *hope* so, Walter . . .

WALTER. (*Furious.*) CAN'T YOU BE ON *MY* SIDE FOR ONCE IN YOUR LIFE?!

RUTH. (*Quietly, reasoning—she will do anything at this moment to avoid provoking him.*) Walter, I *am* on your side . . .

WALTER. Oh, I can see that!

RUTH. (*Gently persisting, crossing to him.*) Honey, will you just listen . . . (*Blind with rage, he instinctively raises a threatening fist—and she halts. A beat.*)

WALTER. (*Viciously.*) WHO *NEEDS* YOU! (*He looks at her and walks into the bedroom.* RUTH *absorbs it for a long moment, and then goes after him. He moves away, to the far* U. L. *side of the bed.*)

RUTH. You want some hot milk?

WALTER. No. I don't want no hot milk! (*A beat.*) Why hot milk?

RUTH. 'Cause after all that liquor you ought to have something hot in your stomach.

WALTER. No, I don't want no milk. Why you always trying to give me something to eat?

RUTH. (*A beat. Simply, starkly.*) What *else* can I give you, Walter Lee Younger? (*It hangs in the air.* Music Cue XII [Score #10]. *He crosses* D. L. *of the bed.*)

SONG: "SWEET TIME"*

WHERE'D IT *GO?* WHERE'D IT *GET* TO?
SEEMS LIKE HERE WE ARE WITH NOTHING
    LEFT TO SAY.
WHERE'D IT GO? HOW'D IT HAPPEN?
SEEMS LIKE WHAT WE HAD HAS ALL BUT
    SLIPPED AWAY.
HOW'D WE *GET TO THIS PLACE*
WHERE WE'RE SCARED TO TALK SOFTNESS,
SCARED TO BE NEAR?
(*She reaches for him. He walks out of the room, gets his
jacket, L., and heads for the door. She steps down into his path
and the two stand confronting each other. Then gloriously—
clutching the memory, reliving each moment as she tries to
revive it in him.*)
THERE ONCE WAS A *SWEET TIME*
WHEN A COUPLE OF PEOPLE THAT I USED TO
    KNOW . . .
USED TO KNOW WITHOUT THINKING TWICE
WHAT TO SAY, WHERE TO GO.

THERE ONCE WAS A *SOFTNESS*
WHEN AN EVERYDAY LOOK HAD A MEANING
    SO *REAL* . . .
THAT WITHOUT A WHOLE LOT OF WORDS
THEY COULD *TALK*, THEY COULD *FEEL*.

NOT SO LONG AGO
THEY WOULD ALWAYS KNOW
ALL THE RIGHT THINGS TO SAY.

IF *I* CAN REMEMBER

*This song should be *acted* with great feeling and urgency: the questions tearing up from the guts, sung freely, rubato, staccato, not rushed;
the memories cherished for all the sweetness and softness that lies in
them; every word and thought sung for its *meaning* even more than
its melody. Musically, the quality should be Black—the Blackest inter-
pretation possible—a cry from the heart with all the subtleties, the
broken lines and jagged edges and, where appropriate, the freely im-
provised quarter-notes of Soul. But none of this for embellishment—
only where and to the extent it enhances true feeling.

SEEMS LIKE *YOU* CAN GO BACK FOR A MOMENT
 OR TWO . . .
AND FROM THERE ALL THE REST'LL BE EASY
 TO DO.
I'M RIGHT HERE WAITING FOR YOU.
 WALTER. (*Turning out, conflicted, as he fingers the contract.*)
WANNA HOLD YOU NEAR.
DON'T REMEMBER HOW.
ALL THE ROADS BEFORE US
GO NOWHERE RIGHT NOW.

RUTH.	WALTER. (*Torn between trying to explain and his own thoughts.*)
THERE ONCE WAS A SOFTNESS	DON'T KNOW HOW TO TRY.
WHEN AN EV'RYDAY LOOK HAD A MEANING SO REAL . . .	DON'T KNOW WHAT TO SAY.
THAT WITHOUT A WHOLE LOT OF WORDS	EVERYTHING I GO FOR
THE COULD TALK, THEY COULD FEEL	IS GOING ITS WAY. (*Drops the contract helplessly on the table.*)

 RUTH.
FAR AS I CAN SEE
YOU'RE NOT FAR FROM ME.
LET ME SHOW YOU THE WAY.
(*There is no response and she starts away—he reaches out and stops her.*)
 WALTER. (*Facing her at last.*)
IF *YOU* CAN REMEMBER
SEEMS LIKE *I* CAN GO BACK FOR A MOMENT
 OR TWO . . .
 BOTH.
AND FROM THERE I'LL BE MAKING IT EASY
 FOR YOU . . .
 RUTH.
I'M RIGHT HERE
 WALTER.
I'M RIGHT HERE

BOTH.
WAITING FOR YOU.
(*They regard each other. She takes his hand confidently and, eyes never leaving his, draws him into the bedroom. He shuts the door, she opens his shirt and draws him down upon her on the bed as the* Music *ends. After some moments* MAMA *enters. She is obviously, excited, eager, calling out for them as she takes off her hat and coat, drops them on sofa, and looks around.*)

MAMA. Ruth—Walter Lee—Travis . . . ? (*Crosses to refrigerator. Hears something. Innocently cocking an ear.*) What you all doing in there? (*A beat. Shaking her head as she crosses quickly to the window.*) Lord have mercy . . . and before dinner, too! (MAMA *picks up her plant as* WALTER *and* RUTH *disengage—*RUTH *reluctantly, clinging to him; he sitting up at last as reality seeps back.* MAMA *crosses to the sink to water her plant as* WALTER *comes out of the bedroom. She turns* U., *sees him and turns away* D. S. *in embarrassment, smothering a giggle. She quickly crosses to the window and puts back her plant as* RUTH *comes out of the bedroom.* MAMA *turns to explain, sees the two of them—adjusting their clothes —and breaks up in spite of herself.*)

WALTER. (*Conspicuously and elaborately surveys* MAMA. *Playfully, to* RUTH.) She don't *look* no different?

MAMA. (*Suspicious.*) Why should I look different?

WALTER. Well . . . rich lady like you . . . Ruth, I think we ought to do something about this right away! I think the first thing we ought to do is . . . make an appointment. We'll wash all that grey away and make a whole new hairdo. Then we'll take her to one of them hinkty reducing salons, you know, where they make you look all— (*Advancing sexily while she giggles with delight.*) young and glamorous— (*He chases her* D. *and* U. R. *of the table.*)

MAMA. (*Breaks up with laughter, then abruptly freezes in mid-laugh and speaks without warning.*) You all sound like you all gettin' ready to LAY ME OUT!

RUTH. Sho 'nuf, Lena . . . why not? These here— (*Striking a glamorous pose.*) rich white women, they do it all the time.

MAMA. Something always told me I wasn't no— (*Imitating* RUTH'S *pose, as she crosses* D. C.) RICH WHITE WOMAN! (*They all laugh.* WALTER *takes* MAMA *and starts to dance—*

whirls her around, and places her in the rocker.) Look out now, boy—get on away from here! Watch out, child—

WALTER. (*Picks up the contract and kneels before the still laughing* MAMA *to show it.*) Mama, look!

MAMA. (*Immediately.*) Ain't no use in it, son.

WALTER. Mama, just read it. It's all different now.

MAMA. (*Not looking.*) Don't need to. (RUTH, *to the right of the table, looks away, unable to bear it.*)

WALTER. (*Desperate.*) Mama, it's a business, like any other business—

MAMA. It's still liquor! (TRAVIS *enters* D. R.)

WALTER. It's all legal. Everything's been put on paper— (*As* WALTER *struggles for self-control,* TRAVIS *opens the front door slowly and peeks his head in, unseen.*) It's all been notarized . . . Mama . . . Mama, I— (*As* TRAVIS *starts to edge behind* RUTH, *she sees him.*)

TRAVIS. (*Lamely.*) Mama I—

RUTH. (*Flaring immediately.*) "Mama I" nothing! (WALTER *jumps to his feet and moves* U. L. *of the table, clutching the contract. To* TRAVIS.) I'm gonna whip your behind! You are one hour late. (*Advancing menacingly on the boy.*)

MAMA. Well, at least let me tell the child something. (*She holds out her arms,* TRAVIS *runs and jumps in her lap.*) Come here, baby. I want him to be the first to hear. Travis . . .

TRAVIS. Yes, ma'am.

MAMA. (*She looks anxiously at* WALTER.) Guess what your grandma gone and done for you today?

TRAVIS. I don't know, Grandma, what?

MAMA. (*Looking at* WALTER *and at* TRAVIS.) She went out and she bought you—a house! (*At the words* WALTER *looks up and crumples the contract in his hand.*) Well, at least it's gonna be yours some day— (WALTER *tosses it helplessly to the floor and moves blindly toward the bedroom. Simultaneously,* RUTH *starts towards him, but he raises a hand and she halts. He stands alone with his back to them, as her eyes embrace him and she reaches out helplessly—not quite daring to touch him for fear that even comforting hands will add salt to his wounds.* MAMA *turns* TRAVIS *from the scene.*) Now you gimme some sugar . . . (TRAVIS *hugs and kisses her; she watches* WALTER.) and when you say your prayers tonight, I want you to remember your grandfather—'cause it was him who give it to you in his own way. (MAMA *hugs* TRAVIS *again.*)

RUTH. (*Advancing.*) Now you get your behind in the bedroom— (TRAVIS *jumps down and runs for* MAMA's *bedroom,* L., *with* RUTH *swatting at his tail.*) and get it ready! (*He exits and she turns back* U. R. *of the table to* MAMA—*radiant.*) So you went and did it . . . (*Raising both hands classically.*) PRAISE GOD! (*She cavorts in jubilation,* WALTER *turns abruptly—and she stops short as their eyes meet.* RUTH *looks at him pleadingly, hopefully, as if by sheer will to make it all right.*)

MAMA. (*Vehemently.*) It's a nice house, too. It's got three bedrooms, two bathrooms and a yard where Travis—

RUTH. (*Almost shouting; a last-ditch effort to breach the walls.*) Oh, Walter honey, *please* let me be glad! *You* be glad, too . . . Oh, Walter, honey . . . (*She reaches out for him, but his eyes stop her cold.*) A home, Walter Lee . . . a home . . .

MAMA. Walter Lee, it do make a difference when a man can walk on floors that belong to him . . .

RUTH. (*Trying to deal with practical things.*) Where is it, Lena?

MAMA. (*Looks away: the question she had been dreading. A beat. She clears her throat nervously.*) Out there in Clybourne Park. (*She starts to rock.* RUTH's *radiance fades and* WALTER *turns slowly toward his* MOTHER *with incredulity.*)

RUTH. (*Uncomprehending.*) Where?

MAMA. (*Much too matter-of-factly.*) Four-o-six Clybourne Street . . .

RUTH. (*Simply.*) Mama, there ain't no colored people living in Clybourne Park.

MAMA. (*A beat. Then, out front, almost idiotically.*) Well, I guess there's gonna be some now!

WALTER. (*Simply, incredulous.*) And that's the peace and comfort you bought for your children today . . .

RUTH. (*Trying her best to absorb it.*) Well— Well—you know . . . I ain't never been one to be afraid of no crackers, mind you . . . but—wasn't there . . . no *other* house . . . nowhere?

MAMA. (*Quietly, turning her eyes to meet theirs.*) No, Ruth, I did the best I could for the money.

RUTH. (*Looks at* MAMA *absurdly a moment, then bringing her fists down with vigor as the radiance spreads from cheek to cheek again.*) Well . . . well! All I can say is . . . if this is *my* time—I mean *my time in life*—to say goodbye— (*She starts to circle the room exuberantly, almost tearfully happy.*) to these Goddamned cracked walls!— (*She pounds the walls.*) —and these here marching roaches!— (*She steps over an imaginary army.*) —and this cramped little closet which ain't now and never was no kitchen! . . . then I say it loud and good— (*Flinging her whole body into it.*) HALLELUUUU-JAH! AND GOODBYYYYE MISERY! I DON'T NEVER WANT TO SEE YOUR UGLY FACE AGAIN! (*She laughs joyously and flings her arms up and lets them come down happily, slowly, reflectively, as she absorbs it all in a long glowing beat of contentment. Then, a glory shout as she turns toward the bedroom and* TRAVIS.) Lord! I sure don't feel like *whipping* nobody today! (*She exits.*)

MAMA. Well, son, I'm waiting to hear you say something. I'm waiting to hear you say how deep inside you think I done the right thing. (*She rises and takes a step towards him. He starts out the door.*) Walter—! (Music Cue XIII [Score #11].)

WALTER. (*Turns back to face her as the lights close in on them.*)

SONG: "YOU DONE RIGHT"

(*With searing, quiet sarcasm—understated and almost offhand at times, as if nothing really matters; and then, at others, swiftly and brutally twisting the knife.*)
YOU WANNA HEAR ME SAY, "YOU DONE RIGHT."
ALL RIGHT, YOU DONE RIGHT!
IF THAT'LL LET YOU SLEEP TONIGHT,
YOU DONE RIGHT!
YOU WANNA HEAR ME SAY THAT YOU'RE SMART.
ALL RIGHT, YOU'RE SMARTER THAN FIFTY
    OF ME.
YOU DONE RIGHT! AND YOU'RE SMART!
WE AGREE!

NICE OF YOU TO ASK ME A THING OR TWO
WHEN YOU GONE AND DONE WHAT I *KNEW*
    YOU'D DO.
NICE OF YOU TO GIVE ME A CHANCE TO SPEAK
    MY MIND!

HOW SWEET, HOW KIND!

YOU WANNA HEAR ME SAY "YOU DONE RIGHT!"
ALL RIGHT, YOU DONE RIGHT!
IF THAT'LL LET YOU SLEEP TONIGHT
YOU DONE RIGHT!
(*MUSIC continues under, timed with dialogue.*)

MAMA. Son, I only tried to do what Big Walter would have wanted . . .

WALTER. *I* could have showed you how to double that money—

MAMA. Son, why do you talk so much about money?

WALTER. Because it's *life*, Mama!

MAMA. Oh, so now *money* is life?! Once upon a time it was *Freedom*. Freedom used to be life . . . now it's money. (*Shaking her head, she sits in the rocker.*)

WALTER. It's always been money, we just didn't know it, that's all. Mama, look at me.

MAMA. I'm looking at you . . . you got a nice wife, a fine boy, you got a good job—

WALTER. A job, Mama? A *job?!* Mama, I drive a man around in *his* limousine! (*With driving, almost exultant emphasis on the "sirs."*)
YES SIR, NO SIR!
WHERE'D YOU LIKE TO GO, SIR?
SHALL WE TAKE A DRIVE
OR SHALL I TAKE YOU HOME?
FAST OR SLOW, SIR,
BETTER LET ME KNOW, SIR.
SHALL I PARK? IS THERE—
(*With all the frustration of the utter absurdity of it.*)
—A MARK ON THE CHROME?!
(*Bearing down now, unrelentingly, as he lashes the "sirs" into her.*)
YES SIR, NO SIR!
WHEN YOU'RE IN THE DOUGH, SIR,
GIVE ME JUST A WORD AND I OBEY.
YES SIR, NO SIR!
WHERE'D YOU LIKE TO GO, SIR—
(Music cuts off. *Abruptly speaking this—to his* MOTHER *as much as to the Man.*)
HOW'D YOU LIKE TO GO TO HELL TODAY!

(Tympani roll. WALTER *turns on his heel and strides from the house*—MAMA *calls out to stop him, rising.*)

MAMA. Walter Lee!

WALTER. (*Turning back to face her, across the silhouetted Southside, as a light picks him up,* D. R. *and another picks her up,* D. L. Tympani rollout. Back to tempo.)
YOU WANNA HEAR ME SAY "YOU DONE RIGHT"?
ALL RIGHT, YOU DONE RIGHT!
AND YOU'RE SMART! . . .
WE AGREE! YOU DONE RIGHT!
YOU DONE ME RIGHT OUT OF MY DREAMS
     TONIGHT!

BLACKOUT

(Music cut off.)

ACT TWO

Scene 1

A Southside Church. Sunday morning.

As the house lights slowly dim and the stage lights increase in intensity, touched by stained glass gobos, the rolling chords of a gospel song are heard. Music Cue XIV [Score #12].

The Pastor *and his plump wife stroll on, from* D. R., *engaged in a quiet family quarrel. She is shaking her finger scoldingly and incessantly when, at* D. R. C., *he suddenly stops her lips with a kiss and, as she beams in gratified astonishment, turns to greet his* Parishioners. *The* Congregation *enters humming, several at a time, down the balcony staircase, to shake* Pastor's *hand, be hugged and kissed by his* Wife, *and take their seats.*

Mrs. Johnson *hobbles in, in her Sunday go-to-meeting best, is greeted in turn and sits on a bench,* D. R. Lena Younger *and* Travis *arrive and* Lena *immediately shows off her new black duster to* Pastor's Wife. *As* Lena *and* Travis *are seated,* D. C., *the* Congregation *begins more soulfully humming the chorus and swaying gently side-to-side to the rhythms of the song.* Pastor's Wife *struts proudly to an upstage seat as he turns,* D. R. C., *to direct his flock (who seemingly also extend into the audience) in song.*

SONG: "HE COME DOWN THIS MORNING"

	Congregation.
	HE COME DOWN . . .
	HE COME DOWN
	HE COME DOWN . . .
Mama.	HE COME DOWN
HE COME DOWN THIS	HE COME DOWN—
MORNING.	COME DOWN THIS
HE COME DOWN THIS	MORNING
MORNING.	

MAMA, PASTOR.

HE COME DOWN TO SHOW HIS CHILDREN . . .	COME DOWN TO SHOW HIS CHILDREN . . .
SHOW HIS CHILDREN THE WAY.	WALK RIGHT IN THIS MORNING

(PASTOR'S WIFE *cuts loose and shouts in her seat.*)

           JOIN US, JOIN US, JOIN US TODAY.
           WALK RIGHT IN THIS MORNING

(PASTOR'S WIFE *shouts again.* RUTH *appears on the* D. R. *stairs. She comes down looking very tired and worried, shakes hands with* PASTOR *and sits to* MAMA'S L., *while the SONG continues uninterrupted.*)

           JOIN US, JOIN US, JOIN US TODAY.

PASTOR.

BEEN A LONG TIME COMING.	WALK RIGHT IN THIS MORNING
	JOIN US, JOIN US, JOIN US TODAY.
BEEN A LONG TIME COMING.	WALK RIGHT IN THIS MORNING
	JOIN US, JOIN US, JOIN US TODAY.
WE BEEN HERE A LONG TIME WAITING	WE BEEN HERE A LONG TIME WAITING
FOR THAT HEAVENLY DAY.	WALK RIGHT IN THIS MORNING, OH YES!

PASTOR, MAMA and SOUL SISTER.

DIDN'T YOU HEAR THAT THUNDER?	LORD, DIDN'T YOU HEAR, HEAR THAT THUNDER
DIDN'T YOU HEAR IT ROLL?	LORD, DIDN'T YOU HEAR, HEAR IT ROLL?
DIDN'T YOU SEE THAT LIGHTNING LIGHT YOUR SOUL?	LORD, DIDN'T YOU SEE, SEE THAT LIGHT—

(SOUL SISTER *jumps up, shouts; a* SECOND SISTER *escorts her back to her seat.*)

HE SAID, "NO MORE   (*Hums.*)
    WAITING."
HE SAID, "NO MORE   (*Hums.*)
    WAITING."

ALL.
HE SAID, "WALK TOGETHER, CHILDREN,
AND I'LL SHOW YOU THE WAY."
(MRS. JOHNSON *is touched by the "spirit," rises from her seat and comes* D. R. C., *where she sings and does a holy dance.*)

MRS. JOHNSON.	CONGREGATION.
DIDN'T YOU HEAR THAT THUNDER RUMBLIN' IN THE SKY?	YES, LORD!
DIDN'T YOU HEAR IT ROLL . . . AHH . . . CRACKLIN' ON HIGH?	YES, LORD!
DIDN'T YOU SEE THAT LIGHTNING FLASHIN' ON BY?	YES, LORD!
LIGHT MY SOUL, MY, MY, MY, MY, MY, MY!	LET THAT LIGHTNING . . . LIGHT YOUR SOUL!

(*She starts shouting and shaking.* SOUL SISTER *grabs her and walks her back to her seat.*)

PASTOR.
DIDN'T HE BRING HIS
    WONDER SINGING
    EVERYWHERE?   YES, LORD!
DIDN'T YOU HEAR HIS
    SONG . . . (WHOO!) . . .
    FILLING THE AIR?   YES, LORD!
WEREN'T YOU BORN
    TO SERVE HIM,

SHOW HIM YOU
CARE?   YES, LORD!
LET HIM KNOW HOW   OH, MY LORD! . . .
YOU CARE! SEE   LET HIM KNOW
HOW YOU CARE!   HOW YOU CARE!

(PASTOR *crosses to* D. R. *stairs to conduct as* DANCE ENSEMBLE *break from their seats into a show-stopping number, while the* CONGREGATION *explodes in a rousing chorus.*)
   CHOIR.
HE COME DOWN, DOWN THIS MORNING.
HE COME DOWN, DOWN THIS MORNING.
HE COME DOWN, DOWN TO SHOW HIS
   CHILDREN . . .
SHOW HIS CHILDREN THE WAY

HE COME DOWN, DOWN THIS MORNING.
HE COME DOWN, DOWN THIS MORNING.
HE COME DOWN, DOWN TO SHOW HIS
   CHILDREN . . .
SHOW HIS CHILDREN THE WAY.
(*The tempo quickens and* DANCERS *cut loose completely, accompanied only by orchestra.*)
LORD, HE COME RIGHT DOWN
COME DOWN—
HE COME RIGHT DOWN THIS MORNING.
HE LOOKED YOUR WAY THIS MORNING.
SOMETHING TO SAY THIS MORNING—
SAID IT ALL FOR YOU TODAY.
(*As* DANCERS *resume their seats,* TRAVIS, *transfixed and unable any longer to restrain himself, gets up and walks* D. R. C. *to address* CONGREGATION, *marching about at the footlights, pointing directly into the audience and, occasionally, whirling about to single out a* PARISHIONER. *At appropriate moments* CONGREGATION *responds with "Amens" and ad libs.*)

   TRAVIS.
DIDN'T YOU FEEL
   HIM, SISTER?
WASN'T THAT MOMENT
   GRAND!
DIDN'T HE REACH
   YOU, MISTER

	CONGREGATION.
TOUCH YOUR HAND?	
AND THE EARTH WAS TREMBLING	AND THE EARTH WAS TREMBLING
I SAID THE EARTH WAS TREMBLING	ALL THE EARTH WAS TREMBLING
AND THE SUN SHOWN DOWN	THE SUN SHONE DOWN WITH GLORY

(TRAVIS *screams and begins to shout and dance as the "spirit" hits him and* CONGREGATION *shouts back.*)

TRAVIS. (*In free testifying style.*)
WITH GLORY YEH, YEH, YEH
WITH GLORY (SHOUTS)
WITH GLORY
AND THE SUN SHONE DOWN THIS MORNIN'
DIDN'T YOU FEEL IT, SISTER?
WASN'T THAT MOMENT GRAND?
DIDN'T HE REACH YOU, MISTER?
TOUCH YOUR HAND?
AND THE EARTH WAS TREMBLING,
I SAY THE EARTH WAS TREMBLIN'

(*He continues to shout and ad lib.* MAMA *raises one finger high in the air to get his attention, but he continues obliviously until, suddenly, he sees her and freezes. A beat.* MAMA *points firmly to his seat; he scoots to it and sits sheepishly.*)

MAMA. (*Trying to hide her amusement, she grandly completes the stanza for him.*)
. . . EV'RY STEP OF THE WAY.

MAMA, RUTH, PASTOR, MRS. JOHNSON.	CONGREGATION.
HE COME DOWN THIS MORNING	WALK, WALK TOGETHER
HE COME DOWN THIS MORNING	WALK, WALK TOGETHER
HE SAID "WALK TOGETHER CHILDREN."	WALK TOGETHER CHILDREN
	EV'RY STEP OF THE WAY

RUTH. (*Standing up.*)
EV'RY STEP OF THE WAY.
ALL. (*Standing up.*)

GLORY, HALLELUJAH, CHILDREN,
BOUND FOR GLORY TODAY.
AMEN.

(At the conclusion, the CONGREGATION *greet each other, shake hands and exit as they entered—except for six who shift benches* U. R. *and sit for choir practice. During this* RUTH *draws* MAMA *aside to a quiet part of the church* D. L. C. *From across the room* MRS. JOHNSON, *the classic busybody, spots them.)*

MRS. JOHNSON. *(Advancing inexorably.)* Well, you certainly outdid yourself singing tonight, Lena. Couldn't hardly hear NO ONE ELSE! Ain't nothing *wrong* . . . I hope? *(Hard of hearing, she cranes her head sideways and cocks an ear for the answer. A characteristic gesture.)*

MAMA. No, Johnson. Everything's jest fine.

MRS. JOHNSON. Well, knock wood. H'you this evening, Ruth? *(Cocks ear expectantly.* RUTH, *preoccupied, does not respond.)* Ruth?

RUTH. Just fine, Mrs. Johnson.

MRS. JOHNSON. *(Peering at her.)* You look a bit peak'ed there. But then I 'spec y'all been working double gettin' ready for the big day. Yessir, I 'spec we won't be seeing much of the Youngers 'round here . . . *(Cocks ear for the answer.)*

MAMA. Oh now, Johnson, it ain't as though we was movin' to Nigeria, you know! *(As* RUTH *draws* MAMA *toward* R. C., MRS. JOHNSON *stops* MAMA *with a hand on her arm and turns her back with a comment. The action is repeated several times through the scene.)*

MRS. JOHNSON. Oh, I ain't signifyin.' I'm just so-o-o *happy* for you all, finally gettin' ready to move on up a little higher, Bless God!

MAMA. *(A little drily, not overwhelmed by the sincerity of the Blesser.)* Bless God. *(*MAMA *starts* R. *with* RUTH—MRS. JOHNSON's *hand forestalls her.)*

MRS. JOHNSON. Oh, He's good, ain't He?

MAMA. Yes, He is. *(Starts* R.*—again the hand.)*

MRS. JOHNSON. I mean He works in mysterious ways . . . but He works *(A beat.)*, don't He?

MAMA. Yes, He does, child. *(*RUTH *pulls* MAMA *away—the hand stops her.)*

MRS. JOHNSON. 'Course you all seen the news about that colored family that was bombed out there in that new housing development! But then I can see the *Youngers* ain't worryin' none! (*Cocks an ear.*)

MAMA. (*Pleasantly—with a determined smile.*) Well now, Johnson, we ain't exactly moving out there to get bombed.

MRS. JOHNSON. (*Enthusiastically.*) 'Course not, honey. Just movin' on up. How's the rest of the family? (*Cocks ear.*)

MAMA. They all fine, just fine. (*Turns to go.*)

MRS. JOHNSON. (*Innocently.*) Ain't seen little Beneatha in church for some time now. Ain't no . . . (*Indicating pregnancy.*) sickness hit her— (*A beat.*) —I hope . . . ? (*Cocks ear expectantly.*)

MAMA. No, the child's just so busy with her schoolin' an' all.

MRS. JOHNSON. Oh, her schoolin'? Ain't that lovely? Lena, you sure got some lovely children. 'Course she ought not let all that schoolin' go to her head just 'cause she's the only one in the family to make something of herself. (*Cheerily.*) Where's Walter Lee tonight? (*Cocks the ear.*)

MAMA. (*Long pause as* MAMA *draws herself up, gives* MRS. JOHNSON *a look, then leans into the ear for emphasis.*) Out tending to *his own* business, I reckon! (*She smiles sweetly as* MRS. JOHNSON *recovers.*)

MRS. JOHNSON. One thing about Walter Lee, he always know how to have a *good* time! (*To* RUTH *intimauvy.*) Don't he, honey? And so-o-o ambitious! I jest *know* it was his idea y'all bought that house! (*Cocks ear. Then, with maximum enthusiasm.*) Yessir, we sure is proud of you all. I bet this time next month your names will be in the papers a-plenty— (*Out front, with left hand upraised to mark off each word of the headline, in the firmament:*) "NEGROES . . . INVADE . . . CLYBOURNE PARK!" (*The hand and the words hang there for a moment as she stares off. Then, solicitously reassuring.*) Oh, now, but don't you fret none, honey, 'cause Wilhemina Othella Johnson will be right here— (*Claps hands.*) —prayin' for you—every day! (*Crosses* R. *toward edge of the platform* C., *then cheerily waves back.*) Bye now. (*She draws herself up and hovers at the edge of the platform to negotiate the step down to the lower level—then exits grandly up the stairs,* D. R. MAMA *and* RUTH *stand looking after her till she is safely gone. A beat.* MAMA *turns out.*)

MAMA. (*To herself, shaking her head with appropriate sounds.*) Mmm, Mmm, Mmm. If there are two things the colored race has got to survive: one is the Ku Klux Klan, and the other is—Wilhemina Othella Johnson. (*Then, as* RUTH *turns to her and she reads the look in* RUTH'S *eyes.*) Child, I'm so glad you come. Better than sittin' home waiting. (*The two sit to talk privately on the front bench,* C.)

RUTH. Couldn't stare at those four walls no longer . . .

MAMA. He'll be home soon, Ruth.

RUTH. (*Urgently.*) . . . It's been three days, Lena . . .

MAMA. He'll be home soon—I know my son.

RUTH. (*Looking at* MAMA *searchingly, almost coldly.*) Do you, Lena? (MAMA *says nothing.*) Lena, Mrs. Arnold called . . .

MAMA. He ain't done nothin'? (*The question is put so strongly it stops* RUTH'S *response and she softens.*) What Mrs. Arnold want, child?

RUTH. She say Mr. Arnold had to take a cab for three days . . .

MAMA. He gonna lose his job . . .

RUTH. (*Evenly, meeting her eyes to make her understand.*) He done lost more than that already.

MAMA. I know it, child. I know it.

RUTH. (*Not convinced.*) Well, I hope so, Lena. (*After a beat of eye contact,* MAMA *rises and starts to leave.*) Where you goin'?

MAMA. (*With determination.*) To find my boy. (MAMA *exits* U. C. *as the silent* CHOIR *rehearsal breaks up and the* SINGERS *rise, chanting* a capella. [Score 12A].)

CHOIR.

HE COME DOWN

HE COME DOWN . . .

(RUTH *rises slowly and exits up the stairs,* D. R., *and* SINGERS *shake hands and prepare to depart as—*)

ACT TWO

SCENE 2

The neon-lit bar materializes, stage L., *and* WALTER LEE *and a* WAITER *enter.*

WALTER, *far-gone, glass in hand, eyes glazed, zigzags into a chair,* D. L., *sprawls over the table and signals for a refill. The* WAITER *pours it and turns to go but* WALTER *reaches out to grasp the imaginary bottle in mid-air and the* WAITER *leaves it, half-shaking his head.*

Throughout this, WALTER *tipsily bellows "BOOZE," while the disbanding* CHOIR, *at* R., *singing in counterpoint, pick up their benches and exit,* U. R., *their voices drifting back.*

REPRISE: "BOOZE"

(Sung a capella.)

WALTER.	CHOIR. *(Singing as needed to cover* WALTER'S *ad lib reprise.)*
BOOZE!	HE COME DOWN
FAITHFUL, FAITHFUL BOOZE!	HE COME DOWN
TAKE A LOOK ALL AROUND YOU	HE COME DOWN
WRITING'S ON THE WALL.	
BOOZE!	HE COME DOWN
FAITHFUL, FAITHFUL BOOZE!	
DIG IN YOUR POCKETS —DUST!	HE COME DOWN
BOOZE!	HE COME DOWN
*(*MAMA *enters* U. L. C.*)*	
THESE UNFORTUNATE MOTHERS	HE COME DOWN
NEED SOME HAPPY NEWS . . .	

(He unstops the bottle, pours a second glass and sets it across from him. Deliberately.) Hey Mama! Have a drink!

MAMA. *(Softly.)* We missed you, son . . .

WALTER. *(Baitingly.)* Just have a drink, Mama— I'm buyin'!

MAMA. *(Crossing* D. R. *of the table.)* We want you home . . .

WALTER. "Home?" *Your* home! Everything belongs to you, don't it, Mama?

MAMA. *(With enormous effort.)* I been wrong, son.

WALTER. (*No, never.*) *You*, Mama?

MAMA. (*Sincere and ashamed.*) I been doin' to you like the rest of the world.

WALTER. (*Cynically, flinging it back at her.*) You ain't never been wrong about nothing in your whole life!

MAMA. I ain't never wanted nothing that wasn't for you. I just didn't understand about the store, what it mean to you—

WALTER. (*Twisting the knife.*) It's "still liquor," Mama! (*He pours another, raises his glass to her, and deliberately downs it with his eyes locked on hers.*)

MAMA. (*Overwrought.*) I know that, son. (*Turns away, out front.*) Oh Lord, forgive me. (*Closes her eyes, sucks in her breath and makes a decision, facing him.*) But I'd rather see you sellin' it than destroyin' yourself like this—

WALTER. (*Lurching bitterly to his feet and starting out L.*) Don't do me no favors!

MAMA. (*Pulling an envelope of money from her bag.*) I made a small down payment on the house. (*He halts listening.*) Tomorrow morning I want you to put three thousand dollars in the bank for Beneatha's medical schoolin'— (*The last straw: with a gesture of dismissal, he starts out, L.—but the next words stop him.*) The rest is for you. It ain't much, but it's everything I got in the world. (*She places the envelope on the table.*) I'm telling you to be the head of this family the way you s'posed to be. (*She hesitates for the briefest moment, then closes her bag and turns to go—too proud to wait for thank you's. WALTER turns.*)

WALTER. Mama— (*He crosses towards her and she comes back, below D. R. corner of table, and he reaches his hands out tremulously, disbelievingly, to touch and caress her face. Simply, quietly, as much to himself as to her: it is less a question than a realization that she does.*) Mama, you trust me like that . . . ?

MAMA. (*Pulling herself together with a supreme effort at composure.*) I ain't never stopped trustin' you. Just like— I ain't never stopped lovin' you. (*She draws her coat about her and exits quickly. WALTER starts after her, then turns back to the money and crosses down to it, U. L. of table. He reaches out but stands frozen for a long moment, hand poised tremulously over the money yet afraid to touch it, while a thousand thoughts race through his mind—until at last he snatches it high with a whoop of joy!* Music Cue XV [Score #13]. *BLUE*

TRANSITION LIGHTS and a triumphant burst of trumpets. He exits, U. L. C., and immediately reappears racing up the U. S. stairs and, as a follow spot picks him up, across the gallery, to swing by the railing down the front R. steps, the money clutched firmly in hand.)

ACT TWO

SCENE 3

The Block and the apartment. That night.

As the backdrop deepens to night colors and gobos cast blue shadows, WALTER sits sprawled on the ground, facing L., his back against the front stoop railing, spent and aglow in his triumph. In the darkened apartment TRAVIS has entered, opened his bed, and now lies asleep on his bed.

WALTER. *(Clutching the money before him.)*

SONG: "IT'S A DEAL"

TIME FOR MAKIN' YOUR MOVE.
EV'RYTHING IS ALL SET.
ONCE YOU'VE TASTED THE PIE
THEN YOU'VE GOTTA WANT ALL YOU CAN GET.
IT'S A DEAL!

WHEN YOU'RE READY TO GO,
THEN YOU'RE PRACTIC'LY THERE,
AND THE TOP OF THE MOUNTAIN IS EASY
WHEN YOU GOT THE FARE.
IT'S A DEAL!
(He gets up.)
THANKS A MILLION!
(Marking off quotation marks and a headline in the air.)
QUOTE ME TO THE PRESS!
CALL ME LATER,
NOW'S THE TIME FOR HAPPINESS.
YES . . . YES!
(Fumbles for his keys, opens front door and crosses D. L. C.)

GOT IT GOIN' RIGHT HERE . . .
GOT THE FLAME TO BE FANNED . . .
AND THE FUEL FOR THE FIRE
IS RIGHT IN THE PALM OF MY HAND,
(*Tosses money up and catches it.*)
IT'S A DEAL!

ASK FOR FAVORS . . .
I WON'T DRAW NO LINE.
GLAD TO SERVE YOU
AFTER SERVIN' ME AND MINE . . .
THEY CAN HAVE ALL THERE IS
'CAUSE WHATEVER THERE IS
IS RIGHT NOW!

NO MORE TOM-TOMMIN' IN THE STREET
IN THE BIG CITY JUNGLE HEAT,
THAT'S THE CRY OF THE MASSES'
RAGGEDY ASSES
TRYIN' TO FIND A SEAT.

NO MORE CHASIN' THE BUGS AND RATS
LIKE THOSE POOR—
(*Enjoying this, quoting the social workers.*)
—"UNDERPRIV'LEDGED" CATS.
LET THOSE JUNKIES AND COKIES
ROT IN THE POKIES,
(*Backing toward the rocker.*)
DON'T REALLY NEED 'EM
'CAUSE I GOT MY *FREEDOM*.
I GOT THE BREAD AND
IT AIN'T GONNA BE MY LAST MEAL.
IT'S A DEAL!
(*Sits in the rocker and immediately springs up again with a final shout of exultation.*)
DIG IT!
(*Flops elatedly back in the rocker. Cut off.*)
    TRAVIS. (*Sleepily.*) What's the matter, daddy, you drunk?
    WALTER. No, daddy ain't drunk. Daddy ain't never gonna be drunk again.
    TRAVIS. (*Unconvinced.*) Well, goodnight, daddy. (*Buries head in his arms again.*)

WALTER. (*Crossing* U.) No, come on, Travis. Get up. I feel like talking. (*Boxing playfully with him to rouse him.*) Come on, Travis, get up. (*He lifts* TRAVIS *out of bed and carries him to the table, sits him on top of it and stands to his* R.)

TRAVIS. (*Groggily.*) What you want to talk about?

WALTER. I want to talk about *you*. Now, what kind of man do you want to be when you grow up?

TRAVIS. (*Unhesitatingly, smiling and proud.*) A bus driver!

WALTER. (*Shocked.*) A what?

TRAVIS. (*Less certain.*) A bus driver.

WALTER. Man, that ain't nothing to want to be.

TRAVIS. Why not?

WALTER. Well, 'cause like it's just not *big* enough, that's all. You know what I mean?

TRAVIS. I don't know then . . . sometimes Mama asks me the same thing and I don't know what to say.

WALTER. Well, pretty soon you're gonna *know* what to say. Hey, man—in seven years you're going to be seventeen years old and things are going to be a whole lot different with us. And one day I'm gonna come from *my office*— (*Winks at* TRAVIS.) and I'm going to give your mama a kiss— (*Playing it to the hilt, living the dream as he spins it.*) and we'll come *upstairs* to *your* room, and there you'll be, sitting on the floor with all the catalogues of all the great schools in America. And I'll say— (*Gruff and authoritative—the All-American Dad of M-G-M movies, pacing back and forth puffing and flicking a cigar.*) "All right, son—it's your seventeenth birthday! Now, what is it you've decided to be? You can go ANYWHERE! You can *be* ANYTHING!"

TRAVIS. (*Imitating voice, manner—and cigar.*) I want to be like you, Daddy! (*A beat.* WALTER *looks away, touched— then nudges* TRAVIS *over* L. *and sits beside him on the table.*)

WALTER. (*Grinning.*) There will always be room in the business! (Music Cue XVI [Score #13A].)

WHEN YOUR DREAMS ARE TOO SMALL
YOU'VE GOT NOWHERE TO STAND.
THERE'S A MILLION AND ONE THINGS
I'VE WANTED TO GIVE YOU—
(*Stands him up on the table and crosses* L. *of him.*)
HERE'S THE WORLD IN YOUR HAND
(*Hands him the globe—*TRAVIS *takes it, tosses it up and bats a home run.*)

AND WE'VE ONLY BEGUN.
(*Taps him*—TRAVIS *sits and* WALTER *sits to his* R., *and puts
an arm around him.*)
IT'S NOT HARD TO SEE
HOW IT'S GONNA BE—
(*Looking out as, with raised hand, he marks off for* TRAVIS,
to the beat of the music, the space on the Great Office Door.)
WALTER LEE—
WALTER LEE YOUNGER—
WALTER LEE YOUNGER—*AND SON!*
(*Father and Son behold the dream for a moment, then em-
brace as the lights—*)

DIMOUT

(Music Cue XVII [Score #14] Underscoring.)

ACT TWO

SCENE 4

Moving Day, some weeks later. The apartment.

WALTER *and* RUTH *are hugging and playing upstage of table,
     while* BENEATHA *closes* TRAVIS' *bed, then takes dishes out
     of cabinet over the sink* D. C., *and deposits them on the
     table, as two* MOVING MEN *enter toting packing cases.*

FIRST MOVING MAN. (*At the door.*) Moving men. Where
you want these packing cases?
     WALTER. Right there. (*Indicates the corner next to* TRAVIS'
bed.)
     SECOND MOVING MAN. Where you want this at?
     WALTER. (*Indicating* D. L. *corner of his room.*) In the bed-
room, in the corner. (MOVING MEN *deposit cases and exit.*
WALTER *closes door and crosses into bedroom to start filling
the cases, while* BENEATHA *starts spraying,* D. C. *As she stomps
suddenly twice on a scurrying roach*—Music cut off.)
     BENEATHA. Now we ain't gonna have no cockroaches hitch-
hiking to Clybourne Park! (*The* TWO WOMEN *laugh*—WALTER,
absorbed in the bedroom, cannot hear them.)
     RUTH. (*Packing a box at table.*) You know what, Bennie?

You know what I'm gonna do the first thing when we get there? I'm gonna fill the tub up to here— (*Marking off the level just below her nose.*) And the first person who knocks—

BENEATHA. . . . gets his head knocked off! (*They laugh.* BENEATHA *puts down spray gun, gets glasses from the cabinet and brings them to* RUTH.)

RUTH. You know it!

BENEATHA. Unless, of course, it's Walter Lee! (*Crossing* D. C., *salaciously.*) In which case you just might invite him in!

RUTH. (*Embarrassed.*) Now, Bennie . . .

BENEATHA. (*Deadpan, as she reaches up for more glasses.*) It's all right, Ruth. I'm going to be a doctor! (*A beat. She crosses to the* U. L. *corner of the table to wrap glasses beside* RUTH. Music Cue XVIII [Score #15].)

REPRISE: "SWEET TIME"

RUTH. (*Looking off, to herself glowingly, joyously.*)
THERE ONCE WAS A SWEET TIME
WHEN A COUPLE OF PEOPLE THAT I USED TO
      KNOW
(WALTER *comes out of bedroom and watches—with a signal to* BENEATHA *not to reveal him.*)
USED TO KNOW WITHOUT THINKING TWICE
WHAT TO SAY . . . WHERE TO GO . . .
(*He sneaks up behind* RUTH, *covers her eyes and she jumps. He takes her in his arms and they dance, cheek to cheek, a close intimate slowdrag, to* D. L. C.)
WALTER.
IF YOU CAN REMEMBER
SEEMS LIKE I CAN GO BACK FOR A MOMENT
      OR TWO . . .
RUTH and WALTER.
AND FROM THERE I'LL BE MAKING IT EASY
      FOR YOU
(*He twirls her out.*)
RUTH. (*With a playful curtsey.*)
I'M RIGHT HERE . . .
WALTER. (*Arms outstretched in a come-and-get-me gesture.*)
I'M RIGHT HERE . . .
RUTH and WALTER.
WAITING—
(*He dips her over.*)

—FOR YOU.

(*They dance on as the MUSIC soars.*)

BENEATHA. Talk about o-o-o-old fashioned Negroes!

WALTER. (*Delighted.*) What kind of Negroes?

BENEATHA. (*Crossing* D. C. *in exaggerated imitation of their dated dancing dips.*) Old-fashioned.

WALTER. (*To* RUTH.) Damn, Bennie—race, race, race! Girl, don't you know even the N double A C P takes a break sometimes! (BENEATHA *and* RUTH *break up.*) You know, I can just see that chick in a few years. She'll have some poor cat on— (*Elaborately seizing* RUTH *in front of the table and leaning her way way back on his outstretched arm to demonstrate.*) —the Operating Table— (*Picking up scalpel like a surgeon poised to operate.*) —and just when she's ready to slice into him, she'll say— (*Very cullud.*) "By the way, my man, what are your views on Civil Rights down there?" (*He starts to slice fiendishly. The doorbell rings and* BENEATHA *opens it—to a middle-aged* WHITE MAN, *hat and attache case in hand, who had entered* D. R. *a moment earlier, looking about for the street address.*)

LINDNER. (*Uncomfortably.*) Uh . . . how do you do, Miss. I am looking for a Mrs. . . . (*He checks a card.*) Mrs. Lena Younger. (*He stops short as* RUTH *shrieks and giggles wildly, playing with* WALTER, *who now has her spread-eagled on the table in a mad kiss.* LINDNER *turns away in embarrassment and the MUSIC stops as* BENEATHA *signals frantically and vainly.*)

BENEATHA. (*Stamping her foot for attention.*) Walter Lee! Ruth! (Music cut off. *As she blocks* LINDNER's *view into the room, enunciating clearly* but soundlessly.) There's a white man outside . . . (WALTER *and* RUTH *look at* LINDNER *frozen for a long moment and at last disengage,* BENEATHA *faces him.*)

LINDNER. . . . Mrs. Lena Younger.

BENEATHA. OH . . . YES. That's my mother. (*Stepping back to admit him, with a final gesture at* WALTER *and* RUTH *as they cross above the table to the doorway.*) Won't you come in, please.

LINDNER. Thank you. (*Takes one step inside—keeping his options open.*)

WALTER. I'm Mrs. Younger's son. Can I help you?

LINDNER. Well . . . yes, thank you. I—ah—understand you people have bought a piece of residential property at . . .

(*Checking slip of paper in his pocket.*) 406 Clybourne Street.
  WALTER. That's right.
  LINDNER. Yes. And—ah—my name is Karl Lindner . . .
(*Hands* WALTER *his card. The* YOUNGERS *look at it, then at
one another, and back to* LINDNER.) And—ah—I represent
the . . . (*Clears his throat and smiles weakly.*) Clybourne
Park Improvement Association. (*A beat. With controlled
anger,* WALTER *takes a step towards him, brandishing the card
almost under his nose, and* LINDNER *draws back as the
lights—*)

BLACKOUT

(Music Cue XIX [Score #16].)

ACT TWO

SCENE 5

Immediately following. The Block.

*Gobo light patterns bathe the set and the stage in the golds
    of late afternoon. A spotlight picks up* TRAVIS, *seated atop
    the staircase,* D. R.

SONG: "SIDEWALK TREE"

  TRAVIS. (*Pensively.*)
SIDEWALK TREE, HANGIN' LOW,
WON'T FORGET YOU WHEN I GO.
I'LL REMEMBER FLYIN' HIGH IN SPACE . . .
(*Slides down the railing to the ground.*)
AND WHEN MAMA'D SCOLD ME,
YOU'D BE THERE TO HOLD ME

(*Slips under the railing onto the stairs again, and straddles the
railing.*)
GIVIN' ME THE ROOM TO CRY—
A HIDING PLACE.
(*Jumps off, runs to the* U. C. *bed and begins to walk a make-
believe tight-rope on the edge.*)
SIDEWALK TREE, NO MORE TIME,

NO MORE SWINGIN', NO MORE CLIMB.
(*Jumps off and crosses* D.)
THEY ALL TELL ME I'VE BEEN THINKIN' SMALL.
(*Sits on the platform edge by the front door.*)
OTHER TREES ARE GROWIN'
THAT'S WHERE I'LL BE GOIN' . . .
WHERE I'LL HAVE A CHANCE TO GROW,
TO SHOW THEM ALL.
(*He starts* U. R. *as though leaving, and then does a sudden handspring to* D. R. C., *and, as he starts to sing again, crosses* D. L. C.)

GONNA HAVE THE GOOD THINGS DADDY NEVER
    HAD . . .
EVEN THOUGH I'M HAPPY LIVIN' WITH THE
    BAD.
With a "thumbs down" gesture, he cartwheels to D. C.)
SIDEWALK TREE, WHAT AN END,
(*Sits on the apartment edge,* D. C.)
GAIN A FORTUNE, LOSE A FRIEND.
BRIGHT TOMORROW NOT FOR US TO SHARE.
GOTTA TRY THE TALL ONES,
WON'T FORGET THE SMALL ONES,
RATHER BE RIGHT HERE NEXT YEAR
THAN ANYWHERE.
(*Gets forlornly up and crosses* L.)
RATHER BE RIGHT HERE NEXT YEAR
THAN ANYWHERE,
(*Pausing at the window to lean out on the railing.*)
THAN ANYWHERE
THAN ANYWHERE
THAN ANYWHERE.
(*Jumps over the* L. *window railing and exits* L.)

BLACKOUT

ACT TWO

SCENE 6

Shortly later. The apartment.

WALTER *is seated on the windowsill, fidgeting with* LINDNER's *card.* RUTH, *upstage of the table, is half-heartedly pack-*

ing, while BENEATHA, *on the couch* U. L., *just sits.* MAMA *enters from* D. R. *with a large empty carton.*

MAMA. (*Surveying them.*) I testify before God, my children got all the energy—of the DEAD! (*Takes off her coat and drops it on the sofa.*) Moving men due here four o'clock.

BENEATHA. You had— (*Perking up, almost gaily.*) a caller, Mama.

MAMA. Sure enough—who? (*Crosses* D. *to pack dishes at the sink.*)

BENEATHA. (*Drily.*) I believe they said they were the Welcoming Committee. (*With a grand flourish,* WALTER *bows and holds out the card, assuming a flat, thin, exaggeratedly Midwestern white accent and tone—Mr. Middle America or perhaps Paul Lynde—which he maintains through the dialogue and the first stanza of the song, and elsewhere as appropriate.*)

WALTER. Yes . . . my card!

MAMA. What's the matter with you all? (*Looks at the card. Knowingly—and without fun.*) Father, give us strength. Did they threaten us?

WALTER. (*Jumping back in mock shock.*) "*Threaten* you?!!" Why, Mrs. Younger! (*Emphatically.*) Not only do we deplore that sort of thing—we out here in Clybourne Park are *determined* to do something about it! We feel—

RUTH. (*Taking her place resolutely to* MAMA'S R. *Same accent.*) . . . that most of the trouble in this world—

BENEATHA. (*Leading* MAMA *to the rocker and seating her with a flourish. Same accent.*) . . . exists because people just don't sit down and *talk* to each other! (Music Cue XX [Score #17]. *The three perch against the table, with* WALTER *in the middle.*)

SONG: "NOT ANYMORE"*

WALTER.
LET'S TALK ABOUT BROTHERHOOD,
  BENEATHA and RUTH. (*Abruptly, they lean into each other in front of him, shoving him back.*)
Hummmmmmmmmmm!

---

*Tempo of this song throughout should be slow enough to permit maximum exploitation of the humor in the lines and the action. maximum exploitation of the humor in the lines and the action. *Resist* all tendencies to speed it up in later performances.

WALTER. (*Breaking through them.*)
'CAUSE, BROTHER, WE'RE MISUNDERSTOOD!
(ALL *nod sharply on the cymbal clink.*)
BIGOTRY CUTS ME RIGHT TO THE CORE.

BENEATHA and RUTH. (*Lean out strumming banjos—and then in, disconcertingly shoving him back again.*)
Mmmmmmm Mmmmmmmmmm!

WALTER. (*Shoves them aside and steps through them.*) ·
IT'S A TIME FOR HOPE . . .

BENEATHA. (*As she and RUTH join him D. C.*)
WE DIDN'T BRING NO ROPE!
(*The three hang themselves—one arm up taut, the other at the neck, head dangling limp.*)

ALL.
NO, WE DON'T DO THAT . . . NOT ANYMORE.
NOT ANYMORE, NOT ANYMORE,
NO, WE DON'T DO THAT ANYMORE.

RUTH. (*Sipping prissily from a tea cup.*)
WE ARE SO POLITE,

WALTER.
WE NEVER RIDE AT NIGHT!
(*He cracks the whip and the three in unison join in horse-whipping* MAMA.)

ALL.
NO, WE DON'T DO THAT . . . NOT ANYMORE.

MAMA. Walter Lee! Beneatha! That kind of talk is just filled with hate!

WALTER. Hate!? We ain't talking 'bout no hate . . .

ALL. (*Embracing the free American air.*)
LOVE IS EV'RYWHERE,
DON'TCHA FEEL IT IN THE AIR?
THERE'S A WAVE OF GOODNESS ALL AROUND.
EV'RY PLACE YOU GO,
DON'TCHA GET THAT BIG HELLO?
(WALTER *and* RUTH *form an arch over the table.* BENEATHA *lounges upon it as in a TV commercial.*)

BENEATHA. (*Gaily waving, breathless, smile fixed.*)
"HI THERE! I'M ON MIAMI BEACH—COME ON
    DOWN!"

ALL. (*With hip, cool strut.*)
REMEMBER THAT GOLDEN RULE,
'NEVER BLOW YOUR COOL.'
LET THE MILK OF KINDLINESS POUR.

Ruth. (*Enthusiastically playing "One Potato, Two Potato" on their fists.*)

EENY, MEENY, MINEY, MOE,

CATCH A—

(Walter and Beneatha, *aghast, stop her from continuing.*)

Walter and Beneatha.

NO, WE DON'T SAY THAT . . . NOT ANYMORE.

Walter. (*Crossing to* Mama *as the others form a Family Circle about her.*) Now we're not rich and fancy people . . .

Beneatha. . . . just plain folks . . .

Walter. . . . who don't have much but those little homes . . .

Beneatha. . . . and a dream . . .

Walter. . . . of the kind of community . . .

Ruth. (*Graciously, noblesse oblige.*) . . . we want to raise our children in.

Walter. (*Reassuringly august, the All-American Announcer—Walter Cronkite, Eric Severeid, You Are There. Or else, Mr. Middle America—flat, midwestern, perhaps Paul Lynde.*) And as for all those terrible incidents that happen when colored people move into certain areas . . . well, I am here to tell you, Ma'am . . . *not in Clybourne Park!* (*They turn and march* D. C., *flanking* Walter, *rapiers raised in salute a la the Three Musketeers.*)

All.

WE'RE A FRIENDLY CLAN

EV'RYTHING IS MAN TO MAN.

THINGS GO WRONG—

(Beneatha *and* Ruth *turn and plunge their swords into* Walter, *who staggers forward.*)

—BUT WE ALWAYS WEAR A GRIN.

(*He chuckles grimly through fixed teeth as the others deftly wipe the blood off their rapiers. Suddenly* All *become mechanical men.*)

THO' THE WORLD IS TENSE,

WE JUST USE OUR COMMON SENSE.

Beneatha. (*Stepping out front blandly, as she takes* Walter's *hand. Southern drawl.*)

"WHY SOME OF MY BEST FRIENDS HAVE SKIN!"

(*Does a horrified doubletake as she turns back and sees the hand.*)

ALL.
WE TRY TO BE NEIGHBORLY,
AIN'T IT THE LAND OF THE FREE?
THAT'S WHAT OUR BOYS ARE ALL FIGHTING
　　FOR.
(WALTER *mounts a chair and the table.*)
IT'S A GRAND OLD FLAG!
　　WALTER. (*Spoken lyric.*)
OH, I LOVE THAT PATRIOTIC BAG!
(*Fourth of July Orator, as* BENEATHA *and* RUTH *march bravely around the table in broad burlesque of the lame, half-blind fife player and patriotic drummer boy of the "Spirit of 1776."*) "We hold these truths to be self-evident: That *all* men are created equal . . ." And that's why we feel that for the *happiness* of all concerned . . . Well, people get along better when they share—
　　ALL. —*a common background!*
　　BENEATHA. (*D.A.R. Lady through tightly pursed lips.*) Race prejudice simply doesn't enter into it!
　　WALTER. (*As* BENEATHA *and* RUTH *kneel, hands clasped in prayer.*)
WE ALL GO TO CHURCH
　　RUTH and BENEATHA.
WE ALL GO TO CHURCH,
　　ALL.
AND WE ALL DESPISE JOHN BIRCH!
(*They rise.*)
WE APPLAUD THE N.A.A.C.P.
(*With forced tepid smiles and the fingers of one hand fluttering soundlessly against the palm of the other, they clap politely, perfunctorily, uneasily.*)
　　WALTER. (*Lorgnette raised, with a trill of false enthusiasm. Spoken lyric.*)
LENA HORNE'S A JOY . . .
　　RUTH. (*Sensuously mamboing down front, Calypso style, spoken lyric.*)
AND THAT BELAFONTE BOY!
　　BENEATHA. (*Joining her, with abandon, spoken lyric.*)
I WOULDN'T MIND HIM *LIVIN' NEXT DOOR*
　　　　TO ME!
　　WALTER. (*As "MATHILDE" strikes up in the orchestra and everybody dances, he unbuttons his shirt almost to the navel and becomes Belafonte. With a shout.*) EV'RYBODY-Y-Y-Y!

ALL. (*Abruptly into street games; hopskotch, jump rope, patty cake, patty cake.*)
WE LIVE ON A FRIENDLY STREET . . .
EV'RYONE KNOWS WHO THEY'LL MEET . . .
EV'RYDAY FOLKS BEHIND EV'RY DOOR.
(WALTER'S *arms arc before him to form a basket—which they pile high with money.*)
WE'RE PREPARED TO *PAY**
JUST TO KEEP IT ALL THAT WAY!*
(*He empties the basket on* MAMA. *Raucously.*)
YOU'LL NEVER HEAR US SHOUT . . .
YEAH! YEAH!
WE OUGHTA BURN 'EM OUT!
YEAH! YEAH!
NO, WE DON'T DO THAT,
(*They line up, one behind the other, and circle the table in a vaudeville turn, arms raised, hands flailing.*)
NO, WE DON'T DO THAT,
NO, WE DON'T DO THAT . . .
NOT ANYMORE! . . .
(*They strike a final pose and· freeze—arms outstretched, toward* MAMA, BENEATHA *on one knee. At conclusion, all three break up completely—with* BENEATHA, D. C., *literally rolling on the floor with laughter.* MAMA *rises, unamused, and stands over them.* WALTER, *the first to sober, tries to signal* BENEATHA—*she sits up, takes one look at* MAMA, *lets out a shriek and collapses again.*)

MAMA. You all through laughin'? (*A beat.*) 'Cause *they* sure ain't. (*Grimly.*) Children, you know what this new house done become?

WALTER. (*Crossing toward her, with great seriousness.*) Yes, Mama, I think we do. (*Abruptly· comes apart in a quivering mass of fear—knees knocking, teeth chattering, hands-in-mouth Willie Best.*)

MAMA. (*A beat. She bursts out laughing, hugs* WALTER. *Then.*) Yes, Wilhemina Othella Johnson— (*Claps loud and clear for emphasis.*) START PRAYIN'!! (*She gets her plant and crosses above table. An aside to* RUTH *and* WALTER *who are hugging, smooching and generally carrying on* U. L.) Now y'all cut that out! (*At table, sticks splints in her plant and starts to wrap it.*)

*These two lines are crucial to plot and *must come across* for only they provide the premise for the action in future scenes.

BENEATHA. (*Snickering, incredulous.*) What are you doing, Mama?

MAMA. Fixing my plant so it won't get hurt none along the way . . .

BENEATHA. You gonna take *that* to the new house?

MAMA. Uh-huh.

BENEATHA. (*In stitches.*) That old scraggly looking no account thing?

MAMA. (*Stops, regards* BENEATHA, *waits for her to subside, and at last firmly thrusts the plant before her. Enunciating grandly.*) It EXPRESSES *ME!* (RUTH *and* WALTER *howl and* BENEATHA *wields a chair in mock self-defense against them, as* MAMA *places plant on* TRAVIS' *folded bed.*)

RUTH. So there, Miss Thing! (*DOORBELL RINGS.*)

BENEATHA. That couldn't be the movers . . . it's not hardly two yet . . . (*She starts for the door—*WALTER *pulls her back playfully.*)

WALTER. Wait . . . wait . . . I'll get it. (*He stands and looks at the door.* BENEATHA *goes to the* L. *side of* RUTH *at the table and resumes wrapping glasses.* MAMA *crosses* D. L. *to the broom closet.*)

MAMA. You expecting company, son?

WALTER. (*Excited.*) Yeah . . . yeah . . .

MAMA. Well, open the door, son, open the door. (*He opens it, elated.* BOBO *stands there, nervously, eyes haunted.*)

WALTER. Right on time, Bobo, right on time . . . Where's Willie, man?

BOBO. He ain't with me, man.

WALTER. (*Gives him some "skin."*) Well, that's all right. Come on in, man, come on in.

BOBO. (*Reluctantly coming inside, taking his hat off.*) H'you, Miss Ruth? Miz Younger. Hey, 'Neatha.

WALTER. You want a beer? You want to sit down, make yourself comfortable or something?

BOBO. (*Still hovering near the door—as close to retreat as possible.*) No, Walter. I can't stay, Walter. I just come by to tell you what happened.

WALTER. Well, lemme hear.

BOBO. Well, lemme tell you—

WALTER. I'm listening, man.

BOBO. (*Trying to draw* WALTER *outside. Half whisper.*) Come on outside, Walter.

WALTER. (*Shaking free.*) Man . . . what happened down in Springfield?

BOBO. (*Almost inaudibly, fumbling with his hat, frightened eyes on the floor.*) Springfield . . .

RUTH. Now what was supposed to happen in Springfield?

BOBO. Me and—uh—Willie Harris was going down to Springfield to . . . we was going to spread some money around about the liquor license . . .

WALTER. What happened down there?

BOBO. (*Half whisper.*) I'm trying to tell you now, man.

WALTER. (*With taut agitation now.*) Man, what is the matter with you?

BOBO. (*With terrible effort.*) I didn't go down to no Springfield yesterday.

WALTER. (*Abruptly drawing him* D. C. *away from* RUTH *and* BENEATHA *at table, and* MAMA, *who stands listening above rocker.*) Why . . . what are you talking about?!

BOBO. I'm talking about the fact that when I got to the train station, man—*Willie ain't never showed up!*

WALTER. (*Halted, life hanging on the moment.*) Why not?

BOBO. I don't know.

WALTER. WHERE WAS HE?

BOBO. I don't know.

WALTER. WHERE IS HE?

BOBO. I don't know, Walter, that's what I'm trying to tell you . . . I waited six hours . . .

WALTER. Now just maybe you was late. Yeah. And just maybe he went down there without you yesterday. You know Willie—he got his own ways. And maybe—maybe he's trying to call you at home right now. (*Grabs* BOBO *senselessly by the collar.*) Now, look, he's somewhere—HE'S GOT TO BE!

BOBO. (*Breaking free.*) What's the matter with you, Walter? You know a cat don't leave you no road map when he takes your money . . . Man, Willie is *gone!*

WALTER. (*Absolute silence, as he turns out,* D. L. C., *away from them all.*) No . . . not with that money! Man, *please,* not with that money! (*Trying desperately to hold on.*) Willie . . . I trusted you, man! I put my *life* in your hands . . . Not with that money . . . not with that money! Man, that money was made from— (*He breaks at last in anguish.*) My father's FLESH! (*BENEATHA crosses blindly to the sofa.* RUTH *sits helplessly.*)

BOBO. (*Moving towards him helplessly.*) I'm sorry, Walter Lee, you know that, man . . . (WALTER *simply raises his hands as if he cannot bear even another word and* BOBO *breaks off and starts out. Near the door, lamely.*) I had my life staked on this deal, too . . . (*He exits and* WALTER, *unable to face them, moves to the sink area* D. C.)

MAMA. (*From above rocker.*) Son, the money . . . is it gone? All of it? Beneatha's money, too? (*Not wanting to believe it.*) Walter Lee?

WALTER. (*Turning slowly to face her.*) Mama . . . I never went down to the bank at all. (*There is total silence.* RUTH *covers her face with her hands;* BENEATHA *sits forlornly, locked in her own thoughts.* MAMA *looks at her son without recognition—and then, suddenly, towards the front door.*)

MAMA. Big Walter. I seen him come in here . . . night after night . . . and look at that floor . . . and then look at me . . . the red showing in his eyes . . . the veins moving in his head . . . (*Quite without thinking about it, she starts to move slowly towards* WALTER.) I seen him grow old and thin before he was forty . . . just working and working himself like somebody's old horse! And, YOU— (*Face to face with him now, she raises her fists powerfully . . . and fights the impulse to strike him.*)

BENEATHA. Mama! (BENEATHA *runs out of the house as the lights crossfade to black in the apartment and up on—*)

ACT TWO

SCENE 7

The front stoop. Immediately following.

As BENEATHA *starts up the stairs,* D. R., ASAGAI *enters and calls out* U. R. *Simultaneously, in the dark of the apartment* MAMA *slowly lowers her fists and crosses to sit in the rocker, while* WALTER LEE *goes into his room and sinks down on the far side of the bed.*

ASAGAI. Alaiyo! I have come to help you pack. (*She halts on the stairs but doesn't respond.*) What kind of mood is this? (*She turns away.*) Is something wrong?

BENEATHA. He gave away the money, Asagai.

ASAGAI. Who gave away what money?

BENEATHA. My brother, he gave away my father's insurance money. (*She comes down off the stairs.*) He made an investment with a man even Travis wouldn't have trusted—now it's all gone! (*She starts* U. R. *He stops her.*)

ASAGAI. I am very sorry. And you now?

BENEATHA. Me? (*Bitterly, crossing to* D. R. C.) Me . . . it's finished! Over. It was all a dream anyhow! A child's way of looking at things. All that nonsense about wanting to "cure" —to fix the bodies and make them really whole again! I couldn't decide whether to go into research or obstetrics! Well, Mama fixed that . . . and my darling brother! Who needs doctors in this rotten world anyhow!

ASAGAI. (*Gently.*) People do.

BENEATHA. (*Impatiently.*) "People"!? Oh, Asagai . . . (*Crossing away to* L. *foot of* D. R. *stairs.*)

ASAGAI. (*Passionately, forcefully—to break through to her.*) Alaiyo, I never thought to see *you* like this! *You!* Your brother made a mistake and you are grateful to him. So that now you can *give up*—throw out the ailing human race on account of it! You talk about what good is struggle! What good is anything!? Where are we all going and why are we bothering—

BENEATHA. (*Whirling to face him.*) *And you cannot answer it!* (*Crosses* D. R.)

ASAGAI. (*On fire. Shouting over her.*) I LIVE THE AN- SWER! I will go home and look about my village—at the illiteracy, disease, ignorance! I will look at the rape of a continent—the wealth of my brothers piled high in the vaults of the West while our people suffer and die—and I will not wonder long. I will fight to change *all of it!* I will give up my life if I have to! (*A beat. He turns her around and says into her face, intently.*) Alaiyo, what I am trying to tell you is this: there is something terribly wrong in a world—or a house —where all dreams depend on the *death* of one man.

BENEATHA. Well, of course there is, but . . .

ASAGAI. Then would it not perhaps be better for you, too, to direct your anger to *changing* that world?

BENEATHA. (*Crossing away,* D. C.) Asagai, I know all that!

ASAGAI. Good! Then stop moaning and groaning and tell me what you plan to do.

BENEATHA. Do?

ASAGAI. Yes. I have a bit of a suggestion.

BENEATHA. What?

ASAGAI. (*Quietly.*) That you come home with me . . .

BENEATHA. (*Indignantly. Misinterpreting his intention and crossing away.*) Asagai! At a time like this—!

ASAGAI. (*Smiling.*) My dear young creature of the New World, I do not mean across the city—I mean across the ocean. Home . . . to Africa.

BENEATHA. (*Turning towards him, stunned.*) To . . . to . . . ?

ASAGAI. (*Raising one hand.*) Not tonight. (Music Cue XXI [Score #18].) But soon, Alaiyo . . . when you have finished your studies—and you *will* finish them—you will find a way as your mother found a way, as your people have found a way—*then*, Alaiyo.

BENEATHA. To Nigeria . . . ? (*Crosses U. to him.*)

ASAGAI. Home. I will teach you the old songs and the ways of our people . . . and in time we will pretend that you have only been away for a day.

REPRISE: "ALAIYO"

LET ME TELL YOU HOW IT WILL BE
IN YOUR HOME 'CROSS THE SEA,
ALAIYO.
(*Moving slowly* D. R. C. *with her as he paints the vision.*)
EARLY MORNINGS BATHED IN THE SUN . . .
WE WILL SEE THEM AS ONE,
ALAIYO.
VOICES RISING
SONGS THAT OUR PEOPLE HAVE SUNG,
SONGS OF THE LAND.
HOW A DREAM
    BENEATHA.
A DREAM—!
    ASAGAI.
CAN GROW FROM A GRAIN OF SAND,
ALAIYO.
    BENEATHA and ASAGAI.
ALAIYO.
(ASAGAI *takes her in his arms and finds her lips.*)

BENEATHA. (*Resisting, half-heartedly.*) Asagai, you're getting me all mixed up— (*He kisses her fully and she responds hungrily, but at last pulls away.*) Asagai, I think I need to sit awhile and think.

ASAGAI. (*Smiling, he seats her on the stairs.*) All right, I shall leave you. Just sit awhile and think. Never be afraid to sit awhile and think . . . (*He backs away, then.*) How often I have looked at you and said, "Ahhh! So *this* is what the New World hath finally wrought!" (Music cut off. ASAGAI *exits* U. R. WALTER *rises, comes out the door and starts* D. R., *sees* BENEATHA—*and hesitates, speechless.*)

BENEATHA. (*Rising in his path, bitterly, hissingly.*) Yes . . . just look at what the New World hath wrought! Just look! There he is! (*He starts quickly past her and exits* D. R. *as she shouts after him.*) Mr. Black Bourgeoisie himself! Entrepreneur! Captain of Industry! Chairman of the Board! (BENEATHA *stands looking after him, and then slowly, in a fog of mixed emotions, starts in as the lights dim* S. R. *and come up on—*)

ACT TWO

SCENE 8

The apartment. Immediately following.

RUTH, *at the table, and* MAMA, *in the rocker, are seated as before. Suddenly* MAMA *sits forward, looks around, rises and starts to walk about the room.*

MAMA. Some new curtains . . . some bright new tie-backs . . . fresh coat of paint . . . Be just fine.

RUTH. (*Raising her head slowly.*) No, Lena . . .

MAMA. . . . And maybe some nice foldaway screens to put up around Travis' bed at night. Why, this place be looking so fine we forget trouble ever come. (*She has moved to the* D. L. *corner of the table.* BENEATHA *comes in.*)

RUTH. Lena, no . . . (*Grabbing* BENEATHA's *arm.*) Bennie, you tell her . . . (*She drags her down across to* MAMA.) You tell her we can still move.

MAMA. (*Shaking her head.*) Ruth, sometimes you got to know when to hold on to what you got.

RUTH. (*The words cascading desperately.*) Lena, we got four grown people in this house—we can work! I'll work—I'll work twenty hours a day in all the kitchens in Chicago! I'll scrub all the floors in America if I have to—and wash all the sheets in America—but we have got to MOVE! We got to get OUT OF HERE!!— (*She is near hysteria and the words hang as she gropes in vain to continue, knowing even as she does that she is already defeated.* BENEATHA *instinctively reaches out to comfort her and* RUTH *turns sobbing into her arms.* WALTER, *who has entered* D. R., *now pauses momentarily outside the door to draw himself together—and enters with forced nonchalance. At the sight of him* BENEATHA, D. C., *turns away, and* RUTH, *too, can scarcely bear to look at him. But if* WALTER *reacts, he conceals it beneath a facade of coolly defiant, almost jaunty bravado. He has made a decision, rationalized a course of action for himself because he has had to. He believes a man must be tough, "realistic." And precisely because he is uneasy with it—is in fact churning within—he can permit no chink in the armor, no doubt or response or awareness of other priorities, to come between him and his purpose. Consequently, he is "super-cool": as the cats in the street say, "JAMF."*)

MAMA. (*At* D. L. *corner of table.*) Where you been, son? (Music Cue XXII [Score #19].)

WALTER. (*Too casually.*) Made a call.

MAMA. To who, son?

WALTER. (*With a shrug.*) To the Man.

MAMA. What man, son?

WALTER. (*On the edge of insolence.*) To *the* man, Mama. Don't you know who The Man is?

RUTH. Walter Lee . . . ?

WALTER. (*Crossing* R. *around table and* D. L. C.) The *MAN!* Captain Boss . . . Mistuh Charlie . . . Oh Please-Cap'n-Mistuh-Bossman-SUH!

BENEATHA. (*Suddenly turns.*) The Welcoming Committee!

WALTER. (*Swiftly.*) That's right! That's good!

REPRISE: "IT'S A DEAL"

(WALTER *flauntingly—rubbing their noses in it.*)
GONNA GIVE 'IM A SHOW!
SING THE HAPPIEST NEWS!
TO BEGIN THE PERFORMANCE
I'LL BOW DOWN AND KISS *BOTH* HIS SHOES.

WHAT A DEAL!
(*Music continues under.*)

MAMA. What are you talking 'bout, son?

RUTH. (*Coming towards him fiercely.*) You talking 'bout taking them people's money to keep us from moving into our house?

WALTER. (*Jaw to jaw—riding over her.*) I ain't just *talking* about it—I'm telling you that's what's gonna happen! (*With a look of desolation, she crosses away, U. S. of table.*) Talking about life, Mama! *Like it is.*

LIFE IS GRABBING THE CHANCE!
LIFE IS CASHING THE BET!
THERE'S JUST TAKERS AND TOOKEN
AND I'M TAKIN' ALL I CAN GET.
WHAT A DEAL!
(*Music continues under.*)

MAMA. You making something inside of me cry, son.

WALTER. (*Supercool.*) Don't cry, Mama. Understand. (*Yet in spite of himself he is beginning to lose control.*)

IT'S THE NAME OF THE GAME!
IT'S THE ONE WAY TO GO . . .
IT'S THE BOUNCING RIGHT BACK
COMIN' UP WITH A FISTFUL OF DOUGH!
(*Music continues under.*)

MAMA. (*Advancing resolutely.*) Son—I come from five generations of slaves and sharecroppers, but ain't nobody in my family never took no money from no one that was a way of telling us we wasn't fit to walk the earth. We ain't never been that poor! We ain't never been that— (*Voice breaks and she turns away a few steps L., unable to continue.*) dead inside! (*WALTER reaches out helplessly; there is no response. He turns to BENEATHA—who escapes to the sofa. He turns to RUTH—who turns away and sits behind the table looking off.*)

WALTER. (*Screaming at them in fury at himself, at them, the situation, the world.*) What's the matter with you all!

DIDN'T MAKE UP THE WORLD!
DIDN'T MAKE UP THE RULES!
THERE'S THE GOOD AND THE BAD,
BUT THE GOOD ALWAYS COME UP THE FOOLS!

DON'T BE WHIPPIN' ON ME
'BOUT THE RIGHT AND THE WRONG!
LET'S STOP COMIN' ON WEAK

WHEN THE WORLD'S ALWAYS COMING ON
    STRONG.
WITH A DEAL!
(*Music continues under.*)
    MAMA. (*Quietly. A step towards him.*) Baby, how you going
to feel on the inside?
    WALTER. Going to feel fine! Mama, I'm gonna feel fine! I'm
gonna look that son-of-a-bitch in the eyes and I'm going to
say— (*Falters and presses on—punishing himself, whipping
himself and his mother.*) "All right, Mr. Lindner . . . *this is
America!* You want that neighborhood out there the way you
want it? You want the right to keep it like you want it? Then
PAY for it!! JUST PUT THE MONEY IN MY HAND
AND—YOU WON'T HAVE TO LIVE NEXT DOOR TO
NO BUNCH OF (*Music cut off.*) —*STINKIN' NIGGERS!*
(*The others turn away and* WALTER, *provoked even more,
lashes back at them.*) And maybe . . . maybe I'll just get
down on my black knees— (*Drops to his knees, a little L. of
D. C., facing out R., three-quarters toward the audience but still
playing it for* MAMA.) and I'll say— (*He starts grovelling,
grinning, rolling his eyes and wringing his hands in deliberate
exaggerated imitation of the Stepin Fetchit stereotype, while
*MAMA, RUTH *and* BENEATHA *watch in frozen horror.*) "Captain, Mistuh, Bossman. A-hee-hee-hee! Oh yasssssuh, boss,
yassssuh, Great White— (*Voice breaks—he forces himself to
go on.*) Father! Just gi' ussen de money, fo' God's sake, an'
we's—nosuh—we's ain't gwine out deh 'n' spoil yo' white
folks' neighborhood . . ."(*It hangs. He turns towards* MAMA.
*Evenly, chillingly and implacably—meeting the full ugliness
of the world in kind—as his eye finds hers.*) And I'll feel fine!
Fine! Fine! (*Music Cue XXIII* [*Score #20*]: *He rises and,
summoning his last resources, forces himself to walk defiantly
into his room—where, once the door is shut, he sinks to the
bed.*)
    BENEATHA. (*A beat. Quickly.*) That is not a man. That is
nothing but a toothless rat.
    MAMA. What you say?
    BENEATHA. I said that that individual in that room is no
brother of mine.
    MAMA. Oh? You feeling like you better than he is today?
You done wrote his epitaph, too . . . like the rest of the
world! Well, who give *you* the privilege?
    BENEATHA. You saw him, Mama . . . down on his knees!

Now wasn't it you who taught me to despise any man who
would do what he's going to do?

MAMA. Yes. I taught you that. But I thought I taught you
something else too . . . I thought I taught you to love him.

BENEATHA. Love him? There's nothing left to love—

MAMA. There is *always* something left to love! And if you
ain't learned that you ain't learned nothing. (*With great intensity.*) When you starts to measure a man, you measure
him right, child, measure him right. (BENEATHA *runs into*
MAMA'S *arms.*)

SONG: "MEASURE THE VALLEYS"*

WHEN A BREEZE GETS TO LOSIN' GROUND,
BETTER ASK ALL THE TREES AROUND.
WHEN THE WIND'S GETTING SLOW,
LOOK AT WHERE IT'S HAD TO GO,
MEASURE THE VALLEYS, MEASURE THE HILLS.
(*Releasing* BENEATHA.)
WHEN A STREAM'S NEARLY DRY AS BONE,
BETTER COUNT EV'RY TURN, EV'RY STONE.
WHEN IT'S ALL RUNNING THIN,
TAKE A LOOK AT WHERE IT'S BEEN,
MEASURE THE VALLEYS, MEASURE THE HILLS.
(*She crosses toward the door behind which lies her son.* BE-
NEATHA *stands beside* RUTH *at the table.*)
WHEN YOU KNOW HOW A DREAM CAN FADE . . .
HOW A MAN COMES TO BE SO AFRAID.
WHEN YOU KNOW WHERE HE'S BEEN,
TAKE A LOOK AT HIM AGAIN,
MEASURE THE VALLEYS, MEASURE THE HILLS.
(*Crossing* D. *to* BENEATHA *and* RUTH *as the MUSIC continues
under.*) Have you cried for that boy today? I don't mean
for yourself, child . . . I mean for him . . . Honey, when
do you think is the time to love somebody the most? When
they done good and made things easy for everybody? It's
when he's at his *lowest* and can't believe in hisself— (*Voice*

___

*It is particularly important in this song that certain words, which
might otherwise be underplayed or run together, be enunciated *unmistakably* so that the meaning of the metaphor can be grasped immediately by the listener. These include: "breeze," "ground," and the
participles in "a breeze," "a stream's," "measure *the* valleys, measure
the hills."

rising almost to a shout and cresting into the song.) 'cause the
world done whipped him so!
WHEN YOU KNOW HOW A DREAM CAN FADE . . .
HOW A MAN COMES TO BE SO AFRAID.
WHEN YOU KNOW WHERE HE'S BEEN,
TAKE A LOOK AT HIM AGAIN,
(*She looks toward* WALTER, *looks at* BENEATHA *and* RUTH,
then crosses D. C.)
MEASURE THE VALLEYS, MEASURE THE HILLS.
(Music out. *As she stands there,* TRAVIS *bursts through the
door excited.*)

TRAVIS. Grandma, the moving men are downstairs! The
truck just pulled up!

MAMA. Are they, baby? They downstairs? (*She sighs and
sits in her rocker. Meeting no response,* TRAVIS *crosses eagerly
to* BENEATHA, *on the sofa, to tell her about the great van—
as* LINDNER *enters. He peers through the open doorway, knocks
lightly for attention, and comes in.*)

LINDNER. (*Hopefully.*) Uh . . . Hello! (RUTH, *the closest
to him, turns her back. He removes his hat. In the bedroom,*
WALTER *sits up reluctantly. To* MAMA *heartily.*) Well, I certainly was glad to hear from you people! (MAMA *turns away
in the rocker, hands clasped, eyes staring dead ahead. He
crosses to the table. Amiably, expansively—small talk to fill
the void.*) You know, *life* can really be so much . . . simpler
than folks let it be most of the time. (*Opens his attache case.*
WALTER *comes to his door.*) Well, Mrs. Younger, with whom
do I negotiate? You, or your son? (*The question hangs.*
LINDNER *takes out a contract and fountain pen, looking from
one to the other.* TRAVIS, *curious, drifts over and abruptly
picks up the papers.*) Just some official papers, sonny.

RUTH. (*Snatching them away and putting them back.*)
Travis, you go downstairs . . .

MAMA. (*Suddenly sitting forward.*) NO! No, Travis—you
come right here! (*Indicating the* D. S. *side of her rocker.* TRAVIS
*crosses. She pats him on the butt and he sits on the floor
beside her.*) And you make him understand about "life,"
Walter Lee. (*A beat. He looks desperately from her to the
boy.*) Go ahead, son. Go ahead. (*Their eyes hold.* WALTER
*takes a step towards her pleadingly, but she folds her hands
and looks off: it is all in his hands now. At last he turns to*
LINDNER, *who has seated himself behind the table and is
studying the contract.*)

WALTER. Well, Mr. Lindner. We called you because—well, me and my family . . . (*He looks about, shifting from foot to foot.*) we are very plain people . . .

LINDNER. Yes. Yes, of course, Mr. Younger. (*Reassured, he buries himself in the papers.* WALTER *continues with great difficulty.*)

WALTER. I mean— I am a chauffeur and . . . my wife, she works in people's kitchens . . . and so does my mother. I mean—we are very plain people . . .

LINDNER. (*Turning a page, not paying attention.*) Yes, Mr. Younger.

WALTER. And—uh—my father—well, my father was a laborer most of his life—

LINDNER. (*Cutting him off somewhat impatiently.*) Yes, yes. I understand . . .

WALTER. And my father— (*With sudden intensity as the anger rises in him at the man's indifference and the position he has placed* himself *in.*) —HE ALMOST BEAT A MAN TO DEATH ONCE BECAUSE THAT MAN CALLED HIM A BAD NAME— (*For a moment he hovers on the edge of violence: if* LINDNER *says the wrong thing now,* WALTER *is capable of anything. Evenly.*) Now do you know what I mean?

LINDNER. (*Looking up, frozen with fear.*) No. No, I'm afraid I don't—

WALTER. Yeah, well— (*Relaxing a little, as he deliberately steps back from the precipice.*) what I mean to say is that . . . (*Crossing around* LINDNER *toward* MAMA *and reaching out to touch her. Simply, with wonder.*) We are very proud people. I mean we came from people who had a lot of pride. (MAMA *starts to rock and to hum—* "HE COME DOWN THIS MORNING" *—as though she were in church, with pride and resolution, her head nodding the amen yes.* LINDNER *is paying absolute attention now but* WALTER *scarcely notices. He has found himself and it is as if the other no longer exists. Near tears, he is nonetheless moving toward an inner calm. He speaks simply, confirming himself and his own.*) And this is my sister—and she's going to be a doctor!

LINDNER. Well—I am sure that is very nice, but—

WALTER. What I mean to say is— (*Crossing* U. R. *of* LINDNER *and signaling to* TRAVIS.) Come here, Travis. (TRAVIS *crosses, grins up at him, and* WALTER *draws him beside him.*)

And this is my son . . . and he makes the eighth generation
of our family in this country—and we have *all* thought about
your offer—

LINDNER. (*Holding out the pen, anxious to get the signature
and get out.*) Well, good . . . good—

WALTER. And we have decided to move into our house, you
see— (*He reaches out for* RUTH *and she crosses to his side.*)
because my father—my father— (*His eyes meet* MAMA's.)
he earned it for us, brick by brick. (WALTER *looks the man
in the eyes and shrugs. Simply.*) We don't want your money.
(Music Cue XXIV [Score #21]: underscoring and curtain
call music.)

LINDNER. (*Disbelievingly.*) I take it—that you have decided
to occupy?!

BENEATHA. That's what *the man* said!

LINDNER. (*Crossing to* MAMA, *contract in hand.*) Mrs.
Younger, you are older and wiser—

MAMA. (*Abruptly holding her hand up to stop him.*) You
know how these young folks is nowadays, Mister. Can't do a
thing with 'em! (*As he opens his mouth.*) Goodbye!

LINDNER. (*Putting papers back in his briefcase, furious.*)
Well . . . I don't know what you people think you are going
to gain by moving where you just aren't wanted and—
(TRAVIS *puts* LINDNER's *hat in his hand.*) where some ele-
ments . . . well, some people can get awful worked up . . . !!
(*But nobody is listening. They are too busy hugging and digging each other as he exits—almost bumping into the* MOVING
MEN *and* NEIGHBORS, *who come on from* R. *to greet and escort
the family off.*)

MOVING MEN. Are you all the Youngers? Jiffy Movers.

MAMA. (*Into action.*) Ruth, put Travis' jacket on him!
Walter Lee, fix yourself up, you look like somebody's hoodlum!

BENEATHA. (*Going to her,* D. C.) Mama, Asagai asked me
to marry him and go to Africa—

MAMA. (*Not paying attention.*) That's nice. (*To a* MOVING
MAN *who has lifted her rocker abruptly overhead—as rest of
the* FAMILY *leave, with the* NEIGHBORS *closing about them to
assist and wish them godspeed.*) Just a minute, young man!
That ain't no bale of cotton! That is *my* chair and I got to
sit in it again, so you be careful with it!

MOVING MAN. (*Frozen in mid-motion.*) Yes, ma'am—yes,
ma'am . . . (*He lowers it gingerly to chest level, turns and,*

*like a ballet dancer balancing nitro-glycerin through a mine-
field, tiptoes out the door— where safe at last, he flips the
chair casually in one hand and saunters off* U. C. *At last* MAMA
*stands alone. She takes one long last look around the apart-
ment, at the walls and ceiling, moves toward the kitchen table,
hesitates, reaches out almost afraid to touch it, starts* D. *and
suddenly is overcome by a sob, which she stifles with her fist.
As she struggles to regain composure,* WALTER *enters and sees
her. He picks up her plant and brings it to her, kisses her, and
leads her out. At the door she hesitates—he turns back for her
coat and, as the* MUSIC *swells, drapes it about her and, taking
charge, with one arm 'round her shoulder, propels her forward.
They exit laughing and joking as the lights—)*

DIMOUT

A NOTE ON FUTURE PRODUCTIONS

I. OVERALL CONCEPT

The script and production notes in this edition, and the floorplans, prop and costume plots which follow, are drawn from the Broadway and National Road productions of RAISIN.

The idea of a minimal physical production with strong emphasis on pantomime and audience imagination was evolved for these productions. *It should not be construed, however, as being intrinsic or essential to the musical.* Nor necessarily as recommended or preferred in all circumstances.

For amateur production, the approach has certain obvious advantages: in cost; in the greater reality that may be achieved through reliance on imagination as opposed to inadequately "realistic" settings whose design or execution may lack the quality to convince; in the fun and challenge of a new technique; and, not least, in the elimination of long delays and interruptions to change sets between scenes.

However, where budget is no object and extensive technical facilities and apparatus for quick changes are available, multiple scene changes and more elaborate effects and settings can, of course, be employed as in any musical, along with full costuming and the like.

II. THE USE OF PANTOMIME

Mime is one of the more difficult art forms, a technique in which most actors have not trained extensively. Its possible pitfalls as well as advantages should be considered.

Sloppily executed, underdone or overdone, mime can be confusing and distracting. But even when performed brilliantly, it will undercut the drama if allowed to draw too much attention to itself—if it is too detailed, too complicated, a disruptive focus for the audience.

Thus, the best mime in a musical of this kind is the *least noticed.* Like fine direction, it should be as inobtrusive, simple and spare as possible; once the initial adjustment has been made, audience concentration should be on the characters and story, rather than on objects and implements, which should register automatically and be taken for granted exactly as they would be if actual doorknobs and dishes were used.

To achieve this will require extra rehearsal: special practice sessions in pantomime, if possible with an expert, to observe and work with the particularity of the objects to be "created," their exact locations on stage and how each functions. (Does the door open in or out, to right or left? How far back does one step from a door in opening it? At what height is the knob? How wide is a whiskey glass? And so on.) Enough time, practice, and repetition, in short, to enable the movements of the company to become so instinctive and automatic that at last the actors are freed to concentrate on the only thing that will really matter when the curtain goes up: character and situation, what is *said* and *sung* and *lived* through.

With this in mind, the director should freely consider whether panto-mime or more traditional means will best serve his/her production—and should feel free, in any case, to substitute "real" props for imagined ones wherever this proves desirable.

III. BACKGROUND MATERIALS

1. *RAISIN Souvenir Book*
For those who may be interested, the photos and related text in this book give an excellent sense of the feel, look and style of the original production, as well as much relevant background data. Copies are avail-able for $3.00 (by check or mail order) from MAX EISEN SPECIAL, 234 West 44th Street, N.Y.C. 10036.
2. *Original Cast Album*
This was produced by and is available from Columbia Records.

IV. HANSBERRY ARCHIVES

The Lorraine Hansberry archives will ultimately be housed in a major university or library. Robert Nemiroff, Ms. Hansberry's literary executor, would be especially grateful, therefore, to receive programs, posters, reviews and any relevant comments concerning local productions of RAISIN. Please address these to him c/o the William Morris Agency, 1350 Avenue of the Americas, New York, N.Y. 10019.

PROPERTY LIST

1 table
2 chairs } all in the same color and simplified block con-
1 rocking chair } struction as the set

Running Prop List—
1 pot and scraggly plant (Mama)
1 partnership contract and pen (Willie Harris)
1 large gift box with 1 large (4′x8′) Yoruba print cloth and 1 headwrap (Asagai)
1 regular size white envelope with check (Travis/Mama)
1 African necklace (Asagai/Beneatha)
1 knock box (offstage for propman's use for door knocks)
1 tambourine
1 roll of paper money (remains of insurance money) (Mama)
1 attache case, pen, business card, contract (Lindner)
6 benches for church (3 to be used later as "packing crates")

ACT ONE
ON STAGE PROP AND COSTUME MOVES

Scene 1—
Walter enters with chauffeur's cap & jacket.
Travis enters with jacket & green cap.
Scene 2—
Chorus members move table & chairs across U. L. to couch, close
Travis' bed, turn rocker D. S.
Transition from Scene 2 to 3—
2 female dancers move table D. S.
Male Dancer moves chair D. S. S. R. side.
Male Dancer moves chair D. S. S. L. side.
Scene 3—
Mama enters with green coat, brown hat, pocketbook.
Ruth enters with purse.
Ruth exits D. L. 1 with green coat, brown hat, 2 pocketbooks D. L. 1
Scene 4—
Man lifts bar and locks it into position.
Man unlocks and closes bar.
At end of trio, Walter, Bobo & Althea get off table and chair.
2 male dancers move table U. L. in front of couch.
2 female dancers take chairs U. L. and put them L. & R. of table.
Willie enters with partnership contract and pen.
Scene 5—
Asagai enters S. R. 3 with gift box containing 1 Yoruba cloth and
headwrap.
Beneatha exits with box and Yoruba cloths.
Travis exits D. R. gets envelope with check.
Ruth puts letter and check in her pocket and exits with it.

Scene 6—
   Ruth moves table D. S., places chairs S. L. to hold ironing board.
   Walter enters carrying sport jacket with contract in inside pocket, brown hat and gold tie.
   Asagai enters wearing necklace, gives to Beneatha, exits with Beneatha.
   Mama enters with green coat and pocketbook.

INTERMISSION
   Wardrobe removes green coat, pocketbook, jacket, tie.
   Crew remove crumpled contract, shift Walter/Ruth's bed into bench positions, bring on benches for church, move table and chairs into position for 2:2, and remove rocker.

ACT TWO

Scene 1—
   Singer brings tambourine on and off S. R. to prop room.
   4 men restore Walter/Ruth's bed to bedroom position.
   2 women exit with bench S. R.
   2 women move both benches into parallel U. and D. S. positions for choir practice U. R.
Scene 2—
   2 women exit U. R. with bench.
   Mama enters U. L. with money in pocketbook.
Scene 3—
   Waiter takes rocker with plant on D. L. 1, places rocker first in D. S. position, plant second on D. S. L. rail. Moves S. L. chair D. S. Takes bench off D. L. 1 with Male Dancer.
   Travis open bed.
   Male Dancer enters D. L. 1 moves table D. S. to mark, moves S. R. chair D. S., takes bench off D. L. 1 with Waiter.
   Travis exits with money.
Scene 4—
   Beneatha closes bed, turns rocker D. S.
   1st moving man places 3′ bench in kitchen, seat to bedroom D. L. wall.
   2nd moving man places 3′ bench in bedroom D. L. corner seat faces U. S.
   Lindner enters C. S. R. with attache case containing pen, contract; card in jacket pocket.
Scene 6—
   Man enters with green coat.
   Bobo enters S. R. 3, exits S. R. 3.
   Mama moves plant from rail to table to Travis' bed which is closed.
Scene 8—
   Lindner enters with attache case with contract, also hat.
   1st moving man carries rocker off U. R. 3.
   2nd moving man carries bench in living room off S. R. 1.
   Mama, plant & green coat off D. R. 1.

COSTUME PLOT

The costumes are reminiscent of the "eclectic" style of the fashion period (1954-61) with an emphasis on body movement. Because both the vocal and dance ensemble perform as characters, as well as scene changers, the need for quick costume changes had to be resolved. To attain effective visual transitions, it was decided to employ the body-suit and body-shirt adding various accessories from scene-to-scene and where desirable completely changing the color scheme.

Male accessories included: hats, jackets, vests, ties, scarfs and "do-rags"—a silk scarf folded triangularly and tied like a turban and used as a head covering to protect processed hair—a style black men wore in the 50's and 60's. Feminine accessories included: wigs (since the Afro was not in fashion); various styles of skirt: sheaf, circular, pleated or biased, which were designed to help change the look of the basic body suit and facilitate movement; jackets, ranging from bolero length to hip length, especially in the church scene; hats made of straw, veil and flowers; gloves and jewelry where appropriate.

The shows basic color scheme was so geared that each principal character wore costumes along one color line, i.e.: Mama (earth tones—brown, rust, olive); Walter Lee (tans, rust, yellow, mustard); Ruth (soft blues and peacocks); Beneatha (various shades of red and maroons); Travis (wine and shades of red); Mrs. Johnson (lavender and mauve); Asagai (indigo and earth brown); Bobo (browns and rusts); Willie Harris (royal blue and purple).

The ensemble dressed in cool colors—tones of bottle green, navy, marine blue, violet and emeralds. The African dance sequence was designed in coppers, gold, whites, blacks, creams, various tones of sepia and brown to highlight the dream quality of the ballet. A great amount of synthetic raffia straw in white, black and tan was used as well as beads and feathers of similar colors for leg bands, armlets, head-wraps, headdresses and great pony tails. The headdresses were made from raffia woven into various tribal designs.

BREAKDOWN OF SCENES

Prologue (ensemble): The Block. Southside Chicago. Night.

Two Groovy Cats
  bright printed shirts
  jackets
  trousers
  black shoes
  "do-rags"
A Young Chick
  flaired skirt
  print blouse
  crinoline petticoat
  heels, stockings
  wig, jewelry

Drunk
  suit
  shirt
  tie
  shoes
Three Chicks*
  flaired skirts
  blouses
  petticoats
  heels, stockings
  wigs, jewelry
 *one wears flaired fuscia coat
Pusher*
  ornate print vest
  trousers
  shirt
  shoes
  wide-brimmed hat
 *flashy style of the pimp
Victim
  flaired skirt
  solid color blouse
  flat shoes, stockings
  ponytail with ribbon
Drunk's Wife
  nightclothes
  slippers
  nightcap or wig with curlers
Little Boy
  pajamas
Male Neighbor
  black trousers
  gray open shirt or undershirt
  black shoes
Female Neighbor
  non-flaired skirt
  blouse
  flat shoes, stockings

*　*　*

ACT ONE

Scene 1: Younger apartment. Early morning.

Ruth
  blue print housecoat
  blue house slippers
  blue head scarf
Walter Lee
  yellow shirt
  mustard trousers
  brown shoes, sox

   narrow green tie
   olive chauffeur's cap
   olive chauffeur's jacket
Travis
  denim jeans
  pallid shirt
  tennis shoes
  green cap
  denim jacket
Beneatha
  print bathrobe
  comical fuzzy house slippers
  hair up in curlers
  face full of cold cream
Mrs. Johnson
  mauve bathrobe
  house slippers
  head scarf
  petticoat

* * *

Scene 2: The Loop. Morning rush hour.

Walter Lee
  (same as scene 1)
Male Ensemble—work clothes (denim pants, worksuits, sweat shirts, hats, caps, sneakers, work shoes, etc.)
Female Ensemble—day-work clothes (skirts, blouses over basic body suits, flat shoes, stockings, crinoline slips, pedal pushers, wigs)

* * *

Scene 3: Younger apartment. Late afternoon.

Mama
  flaired hip length green coat
  brown hat
  brown pocketbook
  print dress
  shoes, stockings
Ruth
  blue blouse
  turquoise skirt
  flat shoes, stockings
  purse
Beneatha
  wine skirt
  wine & white checkered blouse
  red cardigan sweater
  saddle oxfords
  bobby sox
  red scarf
  brown shoulder bag

* * *

Scene 4: A neighborhood bar. Night.

Walter Lee
  yellow shirt
  mustard trousers
  olive stingy brim hat
  brown shoes, sox
  narrow gold tie
  checkered sport jacket
Bobo
  brown cap
  brown trousers
  brown tweed jacket
  blue shirt
  tie
Willie Harris
  royal blue suit
  purple hat
  tie
  blue shirt
  black shoes, sox
Althea
  sexy party dress, cut low
  ruffled crinoline slip
  heels, hose
  jewelry
Female Ensemble: dress-up, sexy dresses, skirts and blouses in blues, orchids, pinks, greens and purples. Heels, hose and plenty of jewelry and sophisticated hair-dos.
Male Ensemble: Trousers, shirts, vests, shoes and sox in blues, orchids, greens and purples. Stripes, checks and solid colors.

* * *

Scene 5: Younger apartment. Next morning.

Ruth
  dark blue slacks
  blue shirt (Walter Lee's)
  blue house slippers
  head scarf
Travis
  (same as Scene 1)
Asagai
  dark brown suit
  shirt
  tie
  shoes, sox
Beneatha
  blue jeans
  blouse

  saddle oxfords
  bobby sox
  head scarf
Mama
  flowered print house dress
  head scarf
  scuffs, stockings

* * *

Scene 6: Younger apartment. That night.

Ruth
  (same as Scene 5)
Beneatha
  African robes
  African head wrap
  (barefooted)
Walter Lee
  (same as Scene 4)
Mrs. Johnson
  lavender dress
  shoes, hose
Travis
  cap
  jacket
  shirt
  trousers
  tennis shoes, sox
Asagai
  African robes
  African head wrap
  African necklace
  sandals
Mama
  coat
  hat
  pocketbook
  dress
  shoes, stockings
Male & Female ensemble: African costumes, see description *Costume Plot.*

* * *

ACT TWO

Scene 1: Church. Sunday morning.

Pastor
  black suit
  minister's collar
  black shoes, sox

Pastor's Wife
  flowered hat
  gray & white dress with jacket
  purse, gloves
  shoes, stockings
  jewelry
Mrs. Johnson
  lavender dress or two pc. suit
  hat with flowers
  elbow length gloves
  purse
  shoes, stockings
  jewelry
Travis
  wine sweater
  white shirt
  tie
  wine trousers
  black shoes, sox
Mama
  black hat with flowers
  black duster coat
  white gloves
  black and green print dress
  black purse, shoes, hose
Ruth
  turquoise dress
  blue coat jacket
  blue pillbox hat
  gray purse
  white gloves
  black shoes, hose
Male Ensemble: dark trousers, light shirts, vests, shoes, sox
Female Ensemble: dress-up dresses, skirts, blouses, frilly hats, gloves,
  purses, hose, shoes, jewelry

* * *

Scene 2: A bar. Night.

Mama
  (same as Scene 1)
Walter Lee
  rumpled yellow shirt
  rumpled mustard trousers
  brown shoes
  sox
  jacket
Waiter
  stripped vest
  shirt

    dark trousers
    black shoes, sox

                        * * *

Scene 3: The Block. Immediately after Younger apartment. Same night.

Walter Lee
    (same as Scene 2)
Travis
    plaid shirt
    denim jeans
    tennis shoes, sox

                        * * *

Scene 4: Apartment. Some weeks later.

Moving Men
    khaki coveralls
    caps
    black shoes, sox
Walter Lee
    shirt
    pants
    shoes, sox
Beneatha
    blue jeans
    red sweater
    bobby sox
    saddle oxfords
Ruth
    blue pants
    light blue blouse
    black shoes
Karl Lindner
    grey suit
    grey hat
    black shoes
    white shirt
    black tie

                        * * *

Scene 5: The Block. Afternoon.

Travis: cap, jacket, plaid shirt, blue jeans, tennis shoes, sox

                        * * *

Scene 6: Apartment. Later.

Mama
    print dress
    hat

  coat
  purse
  shoes, hose
Beneatha
Ruth
Walter Lee
  (same as Scene 4)
Bobo
  brown car coat
  brown cap
  brown trousers
  canvas shoes
  shirt

* * *

Scene 7: Front stoop. Later.

Beneatha
  (same as Scene 6)
Asagai
  stripped shirt
  beige trousers
  light blue sweater
  brown shoes, sox

* * *

Scene 8: The apartment. Later.

Mama, Ruth, Walter Lee, Beneatha (same as Scene 6)
Travis (same as Scene 5, without cap and jacket)
Lindner (same as Scene 4)
Ensemble—two dressed as moving men (same as Scene 4) other males
  and females (same as Scene 2, Act One)

MUSIC CUES

Act One

Prologue—jazz ballet. Orchestra and dance ensemble.

  Music cue #1—Score #1 (House Out) "RAISIN PROLOGUE"

  Music cue #2—Score #1A (underscoring after applause p. 15)

Scene 1—

  Music cue #3—Score #2 "MAN SAY" (Walter—"Eat my eggs?!"
    p. 18)

    Music Out (Walter—"Damn!" p. 20)

  Music cue #4—Score #3 "WHOSE LITTLE ANGRY MAN"
    (Ruth—". . . Woman goodbye for nothing in this world!" p. 22)

  Music Out (Ruth beckons to Travis p. 23)

Scene 2—

  Music cue #5—Score #4 "RUNNIN' TO MEET THE MAN"
    (Ruth—"Here." Triangle cue on Walter's catch.)
    (Ruth—"Take a taxi!" p. 26)

    Music Out (Walter—"Tonight!" p. 29)

Scene 3—

  Music cue #6—Score #5 "A WHOLE LOTTA SUNLIGHT"
    (Begins following blackout as scene transition lights come up
    p. 30)
    Music Out (Mama—"Won't be long 'fore you starts to grow."
    p. 31)

Scene 4—

  Music cue #7—Score #6 "BOOZE" (Music in on dimout p. 36)
    Music Out (Dancers freeze, p. 40)

  Music cue #8—Score #6A "BOOZE" Encore (Following freeze,
    Dancers explode in frenzy of dancing, p. 40)
    Music Out (Handshake and freeze, p. 41)

  Music cue #8A—Score #6A, Bar 70 "BOOZE" Encore (as dancers
    dance off stage and next scene is set by actors, p. 41)
    Music Out (When scene is set, Travis—"Mama . . ." p. 41)

Scene 5—

  Music cue #9—Score #7 "ALAIYO"
    (Asagai—"Well, Alaiyo, I must go." p. 45)
    Music Out (p. 47)

  Music cue #10—Score #7A "SUNLIGHT" reprise
    (Mama—"Ten thousand dollars they give you." p. 49)
    Music Out (As last light dims out p. 49)

Scene 6—

  Music cue #11—Score #9—"AFRICAN DANCE" (4/4 rhythm,
    (Walter—"The Lion is Waking." p. 52)
    4/4 out, 6/8 rhythm starts (as Walter stomps on table p. 53)
    Music Out (As Ruth stops record player p. 53)

  Music cue #12—Score #10 "SWEET TIME"
(Ruth—"What else can I give you, Walter Lee?" p. 55)
    Music Out (As they embrace on bed p. 58)

  Music cue #13—Score #11 "YOU DONE RIGHT"
    (As Mama says—"Walter." p. 61)

(Music cut off into tympani roll on Walter—"How would you like to go to hell today!"

Tympani roll out as spots pick Mama and Walter up at opposite sides of stage.

Walter continues song to end. Music out at blackout p. 62)

Act Two

Scene 1—

　Music cue #14—Score #12 "HE COME DOWN THIS MORNING" (opening of Act II p. 64)
　　Music Out (All—"Amen" p. 69)

Scene 3—

　Music cue #15—Score #13 "IT'S A DEAL" (As Walter snatches up the money p. 73)
　　Music Out (End of song—Walter: "Dig it!" p. 75)

　Music cue #16—Score #13A "IT'S A DEAL—TAG" (Walter—"There'll always be room in the business!" p. 76)
　　Music Out (as lights dimout)

Scene 4—

　Music cue #17—Score #14 (underscoring p. 77)
　　Music Out (as Beneatha stomps on cockroach p. 77)

　Music cue #18—Score #15 "SWEET TIME" reprise (Beneatha—"It's alright Ruth, I'm going to be a doctor." p. 78)
　　Music Out (Beneatha—"Walter Lee! Ruth!" p. 79)

Scene 5—

　Music cue #19—Score #16 "SIDEWALK TREE" (starts in blackout p. 80)
　　Music Out (with blackout p. 81)

Scene 6—

　Music cue #20—Score #17 "NOT ANYMORE" (Beneatha—"exists because people just don't sit down and talk to each other!" p. 82)
　　Music Out (As trio strikes final pose and freezes with arms outstretched and Beneatha on one knee p. 86)

Scene 7—

　Music cue #21—Score #18 "ALAIYO" reprise (Asagai—"Not tonight." p. 91)
　　Music Out (As Asagai exits p. 92)

Scene 8—

　Music cue #22—Score #19 "IT'S A DEAL" reprise (Mama—"Where you been, son?" p. 93)
　　Music Out (Walter—"Stinkin' Niggers!" p. 95)

　Music cue #23—Score 20 "MEASURE THE VALLEYS" (Walter—"And I'll feel fine! Fine! Fine!" p. 95)
　　Music Out (End of song p. 97)

　Music cue #24—Score #21 (underscore music into curtain calls. Walter—"We don't want your money." p. 99)

GROUND PLAN

(FURNITURE, TABLE, CHAIRS & ROCKER ARE IN POSITION FOR PROLOGUE & ACT I, SCENE 1.)

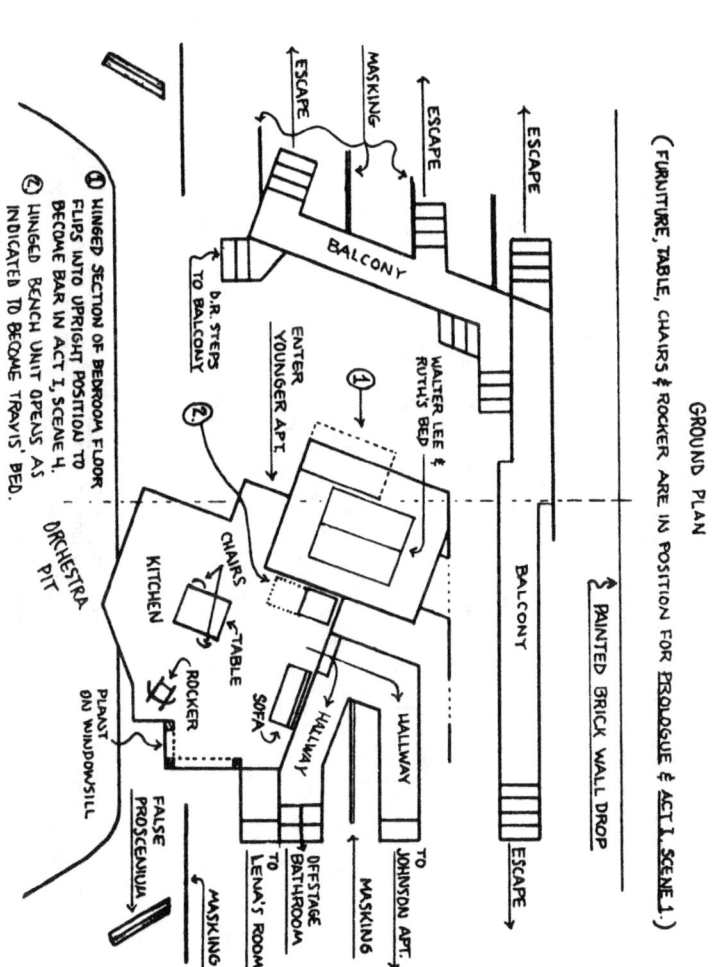

① HINGED SECTION OF BEDROOM FLOOR FLIPS INTO UPRIGHT POSITION TO BECOME BAR IN ACT I, SCENE 4.

② HINGED BENCH UNIT OPENS AS INDICATED TO BECOME TRAVIS' BED.

APARTMENT

FLOOR PLAN OF ~~UNUSED~~ APPLIANCES, DOORS, WINDOWS, CLOSETS, CUPBOARDS, ETC.
(TABLE, CHAIRS & ROCKER ARE IN POSITION FOR ACT I, SCENE 3; ACT II, SCENES 3,
4, 5, 6, 7, 8. STRIKE ROCKER FOR ACT I, SCENE 4.)

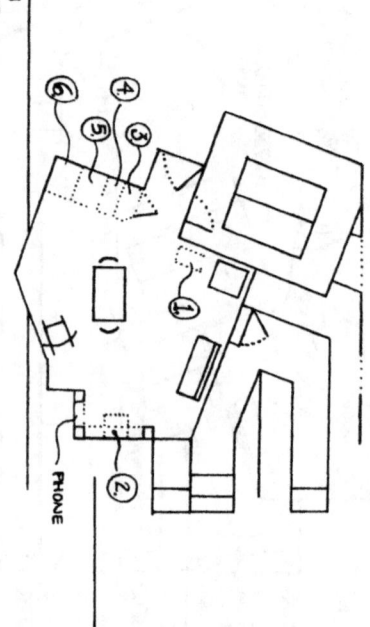

1. PHONOGRAPH
2. ~~BROOM~~ CLOSET
3. REFRIGERATOR
4. COUNTER TOP   { CABINETS ARE ABOVE COUNTER & STOVE
5. STOVE   { & ABOVE AND BELOW SINK.
6. SINK

IMAGINARY DOORS & REFRIGERATOR DOOR OPEN AS INDICATED BY DOTTED LINES.

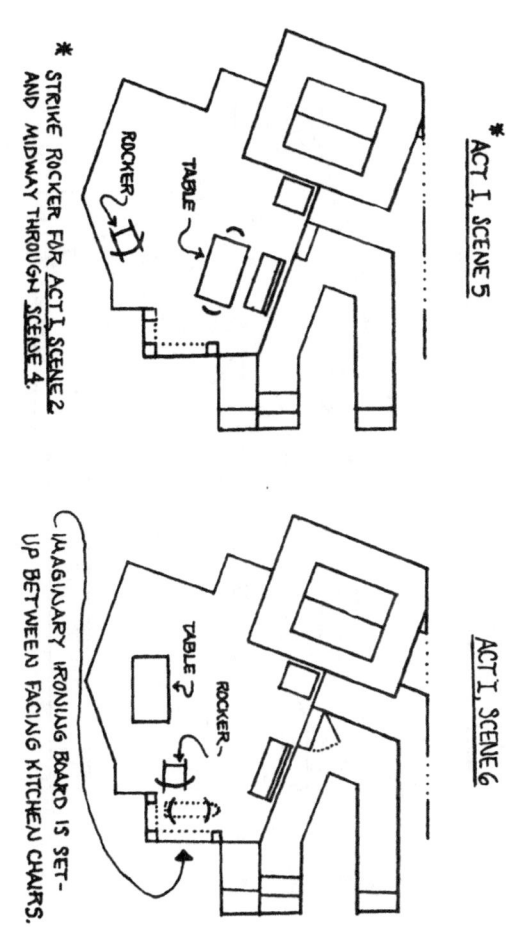

ACT I, SCENE 5

ROCKER

TABLE

* STRIKE ROCKER FOR ACT I, SCENE 2
AND MIDWAY THROUGH SCENE 4.

ACT I, SCENE 6

TABLE

ROCKER

IMAGINARY IRONING BOARD IS SET-
UP BETWEEN FACING KITCHEN CHAIRS.

117

CHURCH SET-UP

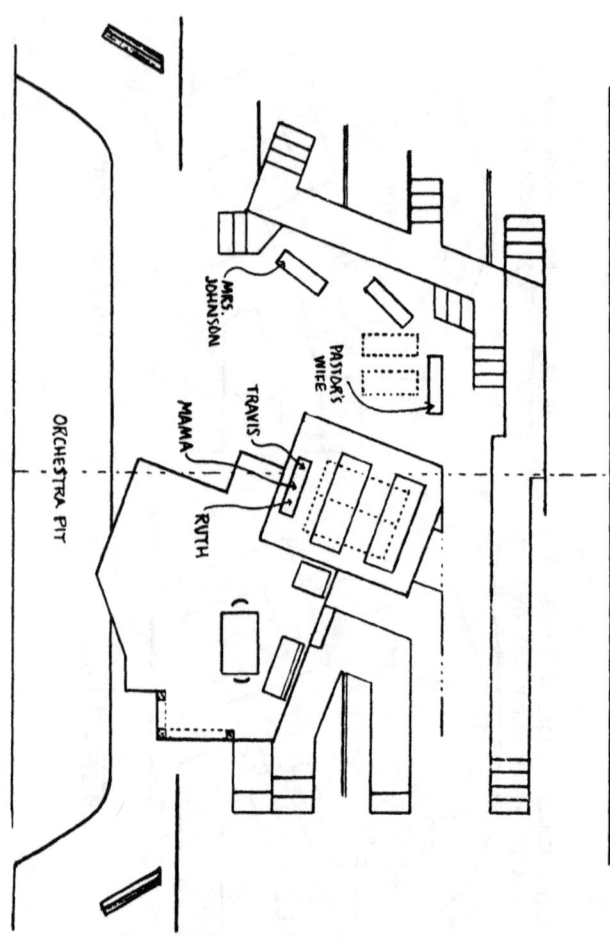

ACT II, SCENE 1 SET BY CREW DURING INTERMISSION. AFTER CONCLUSION OF "WE COME DOWN THIS MORNING" TWO BENCHES ARE STRUCK AND REMAINING TWO BENCHES ARE PLACED IN POSITIONS INDICATED BY DOTTED LINES FOR BALANCE OF SCENE AND **ACT II, SCENE 2.**

ORCHESTRA PIT

MRS. JOHNSON

PASTOR'S WIFE

TRAVIS

MAMA

RUTH